BORN OF MAGIC

HEIRESS OF MAGIC TRILOGY: BOOK 1

H. D. GORDON

*For the lovers
& the fighters.*

The entire city of Zadira stretched out before her, the people filling the streets.

This was the third and final day of winter celebrations, and no expense had been spared. Magic was on full display; fire dancers floated along the avenues, multicolored flames encasing their toned bodies. Sorcerers in capes glided over the gathered, flicking their hands this way and that, sending purple flower petals down in a constant rain until the cobblestones were violet.

Vendors selling savory meats on sticks and fried and powdered dough lined the sidewalks, and various bands plucked out sweet melodies so the people could dance while the children ate goodies and chased each other around the streets, which created a grid among the old stone buildings.

A light snow had just begun to fall, drifting down in lazy white puffs that caught in the hair of the smiling people as their breath plumed out in clouds in front of them.

Overlooking it all was the castle where the princess and her family lived. With spiraling turrets and imposing stature, the castle was set upon a hill on the eastern side of

Zadira. The young Sorceress sat in a bedroom window atop one of the highest turrets as the festivities continued below.

Her Great Tiger, Samson, sat beside her, watching the sun sink behind the buildings and resting his massive black and blue head upon her lap.

"A pence for your thoughts, princess?" the tiger asked, speaking into her mind in the telepathic manner they shared.

Surah Stormsong sighed, stroking the fur between his ears absentmindedly. "I fear something is coming," she admitted. "That war is nearer our doorstep than my father is letting on."

Samson lifted his head, drawing her attention away from the celebrating city below. He licked her cheek with his rough tongue, making her giggle and swipe at her face with the sleeve of her expensive dress.

"I will protect you," Sam told her, his voice a deep rumble in her head. *"Always."*

Surah's violet eyes were already fixed back on the people below. "I don't think I'm the one who will need protecting," she replied.

Samson did not bother denying this.

As princess, Surah would be protected at all costs should the war reach their doorstep. As for everyone else…

Samson stood, his massive body towering over her as he found his paws. *"Come,"* he said. *"Let's save tomorrow's troubles for tomorrow."*

Though she would much rather spend the day in her room reading, Surah knew she would be expected to attend the final celebrations.

Fixing her lavender gown around her legs, she stood and followed Samson through the cold halls of the castle until they reached the lower levels.

They were passing through the main chambers when voices caught her attention.

Surah paused, and her tiger paused beside her, his tail flicking slowly back and forth.

"We'll take your right hand for what you did, boy," said a familiar voice.

Surah and Sam exchanged glances. On the high ceiling above them was a magnificent mural of a stormy sky, a tribute to the family's name. The candles hanging along the stone walls made the painting dance with the flickering light.

"Piss off, you Highborn prick," said a voice that she did not recognize.

There was a grunt of pain and curses from the second voice.

Surah rounded the corner of the hall, and Samson followed along behind her.

Standing at a door that Surah knew led down to the dungeons was Theodine Gray.

As one of the youngest Hunters at eighteen years old, Theo was five years her senior, and already he was as large as a house. With light gray eyes that reminded her of foul weather, and a cruel but handsome face, he was being groomed for a high position in their court someday. Perhaps even Head Hunter.

He was certainly the favorite of the current Head Hunter and her father, the King.

Surah did not share those sentiments.

Theodine and two other young Hunters were gripping the arm of a much smaller young Sorcerer, who was perhaps the same age as Surah. This young male had the greenest eyes she'd ever seen, and dark blond hair that was thick and unkempt.

Surah did not have to ask to know that the boy was likely an orphan, and had been picked up by Theo and the other Hunters for one crime or another.

But Theo snapped to attention as soon as she came around the corner with her tiger. In fact, all three of the Hunters, in their all-black uniforms with Surah's family insignia on their shoulders stood straight and bowed their heads.

"Good evening, princess," Theodine Gray said with a bow, offering a smile she'd only ever seen him adopt in her presence.

"What's this?" Surah asked, gesturing a silk-gloved hand toward the boy.

Theo's lips twisted as he looked at his captive. "He was caught stealing in the square, my lady," the Hunter said.

Surah looked at the green-eyed boy, and he stared back at her defiantly, refusing to even bow his head.

Surah could see that Theo was about to swat the boy for his insolence, and she held up a hand to keep him from doing so.

She approached the boy. He was taller than her, and handsome, if dirty and scrawny for his age, but there was a fire in his emerald eyes that Surah respected.

"What were you stealing?" she asked him.

The boy only narrowed that green gaze.

"The princess asked you a question," Theo snapped.

The look Surah gave the Hunter silenced him.

Surah met the eyes of the boy again, raising her brows.

"Food," the boy said between clenched teeth. "I was stealing food."

"Right," Theo said, yanking on the cuffs around the boy's wrists. "So we'll just take him down to the cells until he can be seen by the committee."

"You will do no such thing, Hunter Gray," Surah said. "I'll take him from here."

For a second, Theo couldn't seem to form words. "With all due respect, princess, he broke the law. I'm just trying to do my job."

Surah lifted her chin a fraction, the challenge clear on her lovely face. "And while I appreciate your diligence, Hunter Gray, I am relieving you of your duty. Take the cuffs off him, and then you boys can run along."

Now Theo looked utterly shocked. "Princess—"

Samson took one step forward. Just one, his enormous black

and blue striped body moving with the grace of a feline predator. The Hunter snapped his mouth shut.

Theodine Gray removed the cuffs from the boy's wrists with a few flicks of his fingers, anger simmering in his steely eyes.

"You may go now," the princess repeated when the three Hunters only stood looking at her.

After a moment, they sauntered off down the hall, and Surah was alone with the boy and her tiger.

"What's your name?" Surah asked.

The boy stared at her long enough that she didn't think he'd answer. But, then, he said, "Charlie… Charlie Redmine."

"It's nice to meet you, Charlie," she said. "I'm Surah."

"I know who you are," he replied, that green gaze still narrowed. "What I don't know is why you helped me."

Surah sighed, though she could feel Charlie studying her. She couldn't blame him for hating her, not when she had so much and he clearly had so little. She had never had to steal to eat, so how could she judge him for his actions?

Of course, that didn't mean that she wouldn't be reprimanded later, when Theo told her father about what she'd done.

She decided Charlie deserved an honest answer. "My family are the rulers of this kingdom," she said, meeting his stare once more. "If young people are starving in the streets, that is a result of our shortcomings, not theirs."

Slowly, as if the words had to sink in, Charlie's face softened, and Surah decided he was all the more handsome when he wasn't scowling.

Surah sighed again as Charlie only blinked at her. "Come on," she said. "Let's go to the kitchens and send you on your way before Hunter Gray gets a chance to go over my head."

Charlie looked at Samson distrustfully, and the giant tiger stared back with golden, unblinking eyes, his tail still flicking lazily to and fro.

"Don't worry," she said. "He doesn't bite unless I tell him to."

In her head, Samson grumbled, *"Don't lie to the boy, love."*

Surah smiled.

As promised, she took Charlie to the kitchens, filled his satchel and pockets with breads, cheeses, fruits, and dried meat, and walked him through the secret tunnels that led out of the castle and into the city of Zadira.

Surah flicked her fingers, and violet magic swirled around her hand. In the dark tunnel before them, the stone wall shifted and revealed a quiet cobblestone street.

She nodded her head at Charlie, encouraging him to go.

Charlie paused, looking back over his shoulder at her. "I still hate you all," he said. "You Highborns are the worst kind of people. Why should you get so much more than the rest of us? What makes you special?"

Samson released a chuff at this, but Surah gave him a look that silenced him.

"I'm not," she said. "It's not fair. I know that."

Charlie scoffed and turned on his heels. "Goodbye, princess," he said.

Surah watched until he disappeared down the street.

"Goodbye, Charlie," she said.

1

SURAH: TEN YEARS LATER

The Sorceress crossed one leg over the other and folded her hands in her lap. "I appreciate the offer, father, but I don't want the job."

Syrian Stormsong looked at his daughter with disapproval, only slightly overshadowed by the grief in his purple eyes. He was silent for a time before speaking, choosing his words slowly, as was his way.

"You are the only one left," he said. "I have a kingdom to run. I would do it myself if I had the time."

Surah's face was impassive, her features relaxed and smooth. She wanted to tell her father that sitting in front of a fireplace in his office all day and mourning the death of his son was not running a kingdom. It was not, in fact, productive at all. He was a man whose only talent was delegating responsibility to others, and she had been doing his bidding her whole life without protest.

But things had changed. Surah couldn't say exactly what those things were, but she could feel the difference all the same. Her brother was gone, and when she had come to her father, asking him for something for the first time ever, he had denied her any assistance. It didn't matter that her brother's murderer had met his end without her father lifting a hand. What mattered was that her father had been *unwilling* to lift a hand, and she would not allow him the guilt-trip he was attempting.

Surah tilted her chin up a fraction, looking at her father with the calm that had taken her years to master, despite the roiling black ocean raging inside her. A black ocean that was the accumulation of a short life with many losses.

Yes, her brother's death had changed things. A final straw.

"This is no longer a place for me, father. I'm afraid I can't accept your proposal."

Syrian's purple eyes flashed with anger, just as Surah had known they would. He may not be a particularly productive person, but he was very kingly in the sense that he was not someone who liked to be told no.

"You would leave our people without a Keeper?" he asked, disapproval now bordering disgust dripping from the words. "I thought better of you, Surah."

Surah's teeth clenched, but her tone was as sweet and soft as always, her eyes indifferent. "There are others with greater control of the magic than I have," she said. "More knowledge and capability, even. I am not the only one who meets the requirements."

The snifter of brandy Syrian had been holding flew into the fireplace and shattered there with a loud crack. The blaze flared, throwing licks of orange on the walls and making shadows dance in the dark room.

Surah didn't flinch, though she felt the heat flash hot against her skin. Syrian hadn't thrown it with his hand, but rather, with his magic, and Surah was careful not to raise an eyebrow at what he would have called a "useless display of power." She loved her father, but that didn't mean her father was easy to love. Over the years his temper had been a constant headache for her, but she had come to accept it as his nature, something that had to be expected if they were to maintain a relationship.

"I am not asking as your father. I am telling you as your king," he said, smoothing a hand through his dark, carefully styled hair, regaining his composure, like the flipping of a switch.

"You *will* be Keeper, and assist the Hunters in their necessary and noble efforts. You should be ashamed that I have to demand this of you. Your brother fulfilled his duty with pride and without protest."

Now there was a hypocritical statement if she'd ever heard one, and though she knew her next words would set her father off like a fireworks display, she said them anyway. She was beyond the point of holding her tongue, which was a pretty distant point. Syrian was not the only one who was grieving, and she didn't need his attitude on top of everything else.

"*I* should be ashamed?" she asked, her calm delivery fueling the returning anger in her father's eyes. She knew she should just shut her mouth, but she didn't. She leaned forward in her chair, her posture straight and perfect, back rigid. "I'm not the one who calls myself a king and yet is too cowardly to seek justice for his son's death."

Harsh, she knew this, but also true. And he had started it.

Syrian's eyes bulged from their sockets and a blue vein pulsed on his pale forehead. His long, manicured fingers dug into the leather armrests of his chair.

"How dare you speak to me like that?" he said, spittle flying from his lips. "You ungrateful child. You think everything is about you. You understand nothing of the world. How is it you have become so selfish?"

Surah was a heartbeat away from saying that *he* had made her this way, but then a knock sounded on the oak doors of her father's study, and a silence fell over the large room.

Surah watched the flames from the enormous stone fireplace flicker across her father's face as Syrian barked for the caller to enter. The double oak doors swung open simultaneously with smooth glides, and in walked Theodine Gray. The heels of his boots clicked softly over the polished wood. His black cloak rippled behind him with each step he took, and his hard eyes spoke only of business. When they settled on Surah, they softened a fraction, and a crooked smile pulled up one side of his mouth.

Surah swallowed to keep signs of annoyance off her face. Theo had never been her favorite person, as he seemed to be everyone else's.

"Princess," Theo said, coming to a stop in front of Surah. He held a black-gloved hand out to her, and she held her own gloved hand out for him, as she had done thousands of times for thousands of people over the years. Theo took it gently and bent at the waist to kiss the leather over the top of her hand, his gray eyes watching her the whole time. "Always a pleasure," he said, then turned to Syrian and offered another bow. "My Liege."

Syrian was not in the mood for interruptions.

"Is it important, Theo?" Syrian asked shortly. "My daughter and I were having a discussion."

Surah could feel the Head Hunter's eyes on her and deliberately stared into the fire to avoid his gaze. She was a princess, and had been for her entire life, so she was used to the eyes of others being on her, and she was good at pretending as though they weren't even there.

Theo had never given her a reason not to like him, had always, in fact, been very formal and kind to her, but she couldn't help it.

But her father trusted Theo, so she kept her opinions to herself. She had learned the hard way that this was usually a wise choice.

"I'm afraid it *is* serious, my Liege," Theo said. His eyes and posture had gone back to business. The seriousness in his voice made even Surah's head turn, and he looked at her when he said his next words.

"We received word from the Dark Mountain. The Black Stone is missing. Someone has stolen it."

Surah's mouth fell open, a rare expression of involuntary surprise on her face. She picked her jaw up as soon as she realized she was doing it, but when she looked over at her father, she could see it was too late. He had seen her horror, no doubt felt it, too. His violet eyes stared into her own, and she could see the victory there. His eyes said this was exactly what he was talking about, why she needed to be Keeper. Why she didn't have much choice.

What Theo said next sealed the deal like a licked envelope.

"Also, Merin Nightborn is dead. Looks like murder."

Surah sighed, sat back in her chair, and thought, *Well, shit.*

2

SURAH

"What do you mean someone has stolen the Black Stone?" Syrian said, his fingers digging deeper into the poor leather of his chair, the blaze from the fireplace reflecting in his eyes. Obviously the Stone was a bigger worry than the death of a royal woman. Which said something. "That's impossible."

Theodine nodded his agreement, then shook his head and spread his hands. "Apparently not," he said.

Surah sat silently, unmoving, even though both males kept glancing at her as though she should have some input. She didn't, at least not other than the same question her father just asked. The Black Stone wasn't supposed to be able to leave its place in the Dark Mountain. Everyone knew that. It *was* impossible.

Also, she'd never much cared for Merin Nightborn. That was a shitty thought, but it was true. Like many Highborns, Merin had always been entitled and obnoxious. Of course, that didn't mean she deserved to die.

Surah's father stood from his chair and began pacing the room, his thick brows furrowed and his head bent forward, thinking. His movements were not graceful or fluid like Theo's and Surah's, but he was a tall, bulky man who moved with deadly precision, and it was rare that he exhibited his anxiety through physical action in front of anyone other than Surah.

This was not good.

"How long has it been missing?" he asked.

"The word was sent as soon as the Hunters realized it was gone," Theo said. "They make hourly rounds to check on the Stone, as you know. The Hunter assigned to check on it at eleven p.m. reported it was still there. When the next man went to check at midnight, it was gone."

All three of them glanced up at the enormous black iron clock hanging above the fireplace. The hour read one-thirty.

"No one saw anything?" Syrian asked, the disbelief evident in his tone again.

Theo's jaw tightened and he shook his head. "No, my Liege. The Hunters assured me no one was seen entering or leaving the mountain. They have no idea how it could have happened."

Syrian snorted. "Wonderful," he snapped. He stopped pacing the room and sat down again in his red winged-back chair, the cushions groaning under his weight. His eyes settled on his daughter. Surah returned his stare with her usual indifference, but inside, she was boiling with questions, and yes, more than a little fear. The Black Stone was one of the most powerful weapons in existence. In the wrong hands it could deliver catastrophe on an unimaginable scale. Syrian knew she wouldn't refuse his request now, and it made her clench her fists in her lap a little, because she knew it, too.

"These Hunters," Syrian said, addressing Theo but still looking at his daughter, "the two that were on watch over the Stone, you questioned them yourself?"

Theo nodded once. "Of course, my Liege."

"And you believe they're telling the truth?"

The Head Hunter considered for a moment, and a small

smile came to his handsome face as his eyes fell on Surah once more. Surah's jaw clenched.

"It would be wise to have the princess question them," Theo said, picking up on the King's intent. "Since we have tragically lost Syris, and that would have been his job. She would know better than I if they were lying. It's not my...forte."

No, Surah thought, *your forte is capture and kill.*

For just a moment, Surah fantasized about throwing a bit of lightning magic at the Head Hunter's midsection. Instead, she sat unmoving, said nothing.

Syrian nodded, giving his daughter a look that said *told you so.* Surah stood in one fluid movement, her long cloak rippling behind her, wanting all of a sudden very much to be out of this room, with the heat of the fireplace, where she had played many a nights as a child, with the eyes of her lost family watching her from the portraits hanging on the walls, with the dim lights that seemed to shadow pain.

"Take me to them," she said, and moved toward the doors without a backward glance at her father.

She would do this task because it was *necessary,* and even though she may only be twenty-three years old, she was not as young-minded and selfish as her father believed. She had lived well as a princess among her people, and she would not abandon them with the Stone missing. That didn't mean she intended to be Keeper, just that she could help in this matter and she would. And, hopefully, it would turn out to be a misunderstanding. Once it got straightened out, she would take her leave, even though she had no idea where she'd even go. Just...*away.* Someplace without old fireplaces and portraits and shadows.

Theo bowed once more to his king and followed Surah out into the hallway, shutting the oak doors behind him with a small flick of his wrist.

"It's very generous for you to offer your assistance, princess," he said, holding an elbow out to her.

Despite her dislike of him, Surah laced her arm through his so he could lead her out of her father's quarters, where they would be able to portal to their destination. For protection reasons, one could not portal into Syrian's dwellings, only out. And though Surah would rather not make physical contact with the Head Hunter, she knew well enough what was expected of her. Theodine was the Head Hunter, and to disrespect him by refusing his arm would be plainly rude. It was one of the reasons she dreamed of leaving this place, even though she knew she could never live any more lavishly than she did in her father's castle. Too many appearances to hold up. Too many expectations. Too many secrets and sad times between these walls.

The hallway was dimly lit; no windows or points of entry save for the two arched doors at the end of the hall. Surah did not respond to Theo's comment about her generosity. She got the feeling that he knew as well as she did that he had not given her much choice with his charging in and saying how she was needed to question the Hunters, probably to help solve the murder, too. It was an understandable request. One of Surah's gifts, that both her lost sister and brother had shared, was being able to detect lies from most people, but that didn't mean she liked the way Theo had pulled her into this. She didn't like it at all.

Theo's wrist flicked again and the arched doors leading to the foyer swung open. The foyer was a large room, one of many in the beast of a structure that was her father's castle. The ceiling towered thirty feet overhead, painted with a mural of a dark storm just rolling in. The bruised clouds seemed to sweep over the ceiling as if to swallow it, and the room was as poorly lit as the hallway they'd just emerged from. But the mural was no longer a comfort to Surah, just like the thick stone walls which held no windows were no longer, even though they used to be when she was a little girl. She could still remember when it had been painted. She'd been only a handful of years old at the time. Syris and Syra had stood to either side of her, their necks craned back the same as hers.

"It looks like it could pour rain down on us at any second," Syris had said.

His sisters had nodded, wide purple eyes still glued to the ceiling. Syra had leaned in a little, pitching her voice low so that the artist still finishing the mural wouldn't hear her. *"I don't like it,"* she'd said.

Surah had smiled at her older sister. *"I do."*

"May I inquire something, princess?" Theo asked, pulling Surah out of her memories.

Surah restrained a sigh and nodded. People were always asking permission to "inquire" things, as though she weren't as accessible as any of them just because she was princess, the next and only person in line to the throne. No one just spoke freely to her like she was a real person. Now that Syris was gone, her father was the only one left who said whatever he felt to her. She wondered briefly if her life would always be that way. It was a surprisingly sad little thought.

Theo's eyes were on her. She could feel them.

"Are you going to accept the position as Keeper?" he asked.

She lied without hesitation, smoothly. "I don't know."

Theo was silent for a moment, his hand resting on hers where she had her arm laced through his.

"It would make me very happy if you did, my lady," Theo said, his tone pitching low, his gray eyes lowering in a rare show of uncertainty.

When he said things like this, which he did a good portion of the time, Surah felt bad about her dislike of him. He was, after all, a Hunter who had fought for her father and done his bidding since he was a boy. She had known him since they were both children, and nearly every eligible woman in the kingdom would cut off a finger to be with him. Handsome, charming, intelligent, strong. It wasn't hard to see why. But, still…

Surah smiled her practiced smile. It wasn't difficult. "Thank you, Hunter Gray," she said. "I suppose we shall just have to see."

He had never, in all the years they'd known each other, asked her to call him Theo, but she knew he wished she would. She never did, not because she wanted to upset him, but because she felt as though he was just waiting for that kind of invitation, and she had no desire to encourage him.

Theo said nothing to this, only continued to look down at her from his taller position. Surah decided it would be best to get back to the business at hand. "Where are we going?" she asked.

It was a question she already knew the answer to, and Theo knew this, but he answered dutifully, letting the subject drop.

"The Hunters who are stationed at Black Mountain are not allowed to leave their posts, my lady, so the two that were on watch tonight are waiting for us there."

They were across the large foyer now, where five Hunters were guarding the portal room. They stood silent in their black cloaks, arms at their sides and faces unmoving. Two on each side of the door to the room, and one directly in front of it. Theo nodded to the one in the middle, and the Hunter twisted his wrist, and the door slid open. Then he stepped to the side so Surah and Theo could enter, bowing as they passed.

It was just a small, square room, not much bigger than an elevator, the walls and ceiling all black, with a plush purple carpet on the floor. This was one of only five places in the castle where portals weren't blocked, and they could only be used two at a time. Surah and her father were the only ones who were allowed to portal freely in the castle.

In front of them, the door slid closed. Much later, Surah would wish she had never stepped into the room in the first place. Had she stuck to her guns, and refused a hand in all this, so much could have been avoided. Maybe.

Theodine held out a hand to the princess, a crooked smile on his face that made Surah sigh mentally. She didn't need the help portaling any more than she needed the help walking, but there were those pesky expectations; *obligations*, really, so she placed her hand in his without hesitation, offering her royal smile as she did so.

Someday I will shed the mask, she thought. *Someday.*

3

———————

SURAH

Traveling by portal would be a strange thing for a first-timer, and most people could never even do it, but Surah had learned and mastered the magic when she had been just a child, so the feeling of vertigo and nausea no longer invaded her as they moved across space and time. She was here, and then she was there. Simple as that.

The night stars hung overhead, a thick glitter that was not visible in the part of her father's kingdom where she called home. Too many lights on the ground to see the lights in sky.

But here was country, a land where only the farmers and their grasses, the Hunters and their mountain lived. Here was a land where the beasts still roamed in the forests, where the night wind whispered the wishes of star-crossed lovers, where the magic was still used for survival, not show or pride.

Here was where the stars were allowed to shine.

She had only been here a handful of times, as her life and duties demanded most of her time be spent in Zadira, where her father's castle was. But sometimes she dreamed of this land, could see it through the eyes of a broken young girl, could see her sister's face as it had been so many years ago.

Battles of the first Great War had been fought here, back before the dividing of the Territories, and it was fair to say the land had acquired a haunted feel, as so many places where great death is wrought do. Surah knew this was the reason her father had built his city on the other large expanse of land that belonged to the Sorcerers, but even with the memories of Syra and her mother, she liked it here. Things were simpler here. You could see the stars.

Ahead was the Dark Mountain, living up to its name under the black, glittering sky. The towering peaks seemed not to hold shadows, but rather to birth them, and rather than hanging over the mountain, perpetual storm clouds churned around it. Jutting rocks the color of midnight scraped the air some twenty-thousand feet high, and a base for the Hunters who guarded the place was just a row of squat black buildings at the foot of it.

A cast iron fence ringed the area, where admittance was only allowed to a select few. The place was as impenetrable as a place could be, and for good reason. The Dark Mountain was where the Black Stone lived, or where it *had* lived, before it had gone missing—which Surah still hoped was some sort of stupid mistake. *She* couldn't even steal the Stone if she wanted to, and not only was she the princess, but she was more powerful than most when it came to the magic.

If it was indeed gone, great trouble lay ahead. The Black Stone, unlike its sister, the White Stone, could be used only for black magic, for bad deeds. In nearly a thousand years, she had never even seen the thing, nor would she want to.

Only the people who guarded it saw it, which was why this interrogation would not be a pleasant thing. Prolonged exposure to the Stone had a way of…shaping a person.

Theo still held her hand and he began walking her over the rich green grasses toward the mountain. She slipped her arm through his when he offered his elbow again, and ignored the tightening of her stomach the way she had learned to ignore most emotional impulses over the years.

"Don't be afraid, my lady," Theodine said, looking down at her with his crooked grin.

Surah didn't respond to this. She stared straight ahead and clenched her teeth. The pride that she felt the need to assert when she was younger had faded away along with the rest of the things that fade away with time.

He led her toward the gates where two Hunters in their black cloaks stood to either side, their faces as stone as the mountain that loomed behind them. They recognized the Head Hunter and their princess immediately and bowed first to Surah, and then him. Theo inclined his head and the gates swung open, stirring the humid air that had caused a thin fog to settle over the land.

Surah's black hood was drawn up over her head, hiding her lavender hair from view and casting much of her smooth face in shadows. The Hunters here, all male, had not seen a female in Gods knew how long. They made great sacrifices for their people, and she did not want to entice them unnecessarily.

The two of them, arm in arm, crossed the land that had gone barren under their feet, the grasses ending abruptly in dry brown dirt. They approached the foot of the Dark Mountain, which seemed to pulse something that made Surah's heart quicken and her breath fall short.

Somehow, though the settings were as different as could be, the feel of the place had the same as that of the Silver City that belonged to the Vampires and Wolves after she had watched their revolution take place there. The air here was warm, not frigid and cold, and the Mountain was dark like its name, not all white and silver with snow, as the Silver City had been, but the *feel* was the same. Darkness. Pain. Death.

Surah nodded to all the Hunters they passed, who nodded in return and followed her with eyes that hung in the shadows of their hoods. As they reached an opening in the Mountain, five Hunters guarding the entrance stepped to the side, allowing them to pass, allowing the Mountain to swallow them.

There were no shadows in here, for not even shadows could live in such complete darkness. After a few moments in the void of blackness, Theo snapped his fingers and a sphere of light, an apple-sized thing that swirled perpetually like the eye of a hurricane, appeared in front of them.

"Where are they?" she asked, deciding the silence between the two of them was too much in this small, dark space.

Too *intimate.*

Theo nodded his head forward, sending the light sphere down the tunnel ahead of them. The shadows scuttled away from it like insects.

"Just around that bend, my lady. They've prepared a room for us. The Hunters who last saw the Stone will be there."

Surah had already begun to move forward, dropping Theo's arm to walk independently, ignoring the look he gave her as she did so.

When they reached the room—which was no more than a small rounded cavern with three burning torches hanging on the wall—they found the two Hunters in question seated at a small, old table. It just barely fit in the small space with its four chairs. The two chairs opposite the Hunters were empty, and Surah inclined her head, using her magic to make one slide back from the table before Theo could pull it out for her. She took a seat. Theo stood a moment, then did the same.

Surah pushed her cloak off her head, revealing her lavender curls. She raised her chin, her violet eyes settling on the Hunters. "I am Surah Stormsong," she said.

Both Hunters nodded in unison, obviously aware of who she was, and said, "My lady."

"May I have your names, sirs?"

Both males were stocky and wide-shouldered. Their hair

was cut close and their eyes were black, like midnight and ink, as were all the Hunters' stationed at the Dark Mountain. Working so close to the Black Stone had its effects, but it was a necessary and honorable duty to uphold. Whether they were suspect or not, they deserved their princess's respect.

The one on the left answered first. "Rand Fishwell," he said.

Surah nodded. Common name.

The one on the right said, "Brim Ironwater."

Another nod, slightly less common name.

"Can you tell me what happened Sir Fishwell, Sir Ironwater?" she asked.

"Wish there was more to tell, my lady," said Fishwell. "I went in at eleven to check on the Stone and it was there." His black eyes flicked to the other Hunter. "When Ironwater went in at midnight, it was gone."

Surah sat back in her chair, sure to keep the dread of what she had to do next off her face. She slid the glove off her right hand.

"May I ask you a question, princess?" said Ironwater.

Theo shot the Hunter a glare, and Surah decided she liked Ironwater for not flinching.

Surah nodded, curious. "Of course."

"Are you going to be the new Keeper?"

She smiled politely. On second thought, she should have declined his request. "That matter has not been decided, sir," she said, and placed her ungloved right hand on the table, palm up.

Ironwater sighed and placed his rough hand in hers.

Surah took a deep, silent breath and let it out. She could already feel the darkness in the Hunter that was a result of years spent near the Black Stone. It was a feeling that quite simply sucked the light out of the world.

"Now tell me again, please," she said.

Ironwater nodded. He repeated the story that Fishwell had told. Surah's sixth sense revealed that he was telling the truth.

She released her hold on his hand and patted it gently, then offered hers to Fishwell.

Same story. Same results. The two Hunters were telling the truth.

Surah sat back in her chair once more, giving Theo a nod that confirmed their stories. She bit the inside of her bottom lip a little as she wondered what she was supposed to do next, and wished for what seemed like the thousandth time in the past month that her brother were here. Keeper was Syris's job, and he had been good at it. She hadn't the slightest clue as to how to lead an investigation of this magnitude, or any magnitude, for that matter.

She had a feeling it was going to be a very long day.

"The room that held the Stone," she said. "Has it been searched?"

Theo answered. "Of course, my lady. I searched it myself before I came to King Syrian. There is nothing there."

The way he said this made Surah's back rise a little, as though this were a silly question, as if to point out that she didn't know what she was doing. Or maybe she was just defensive because she *didn't* know what she was doing. There had been no implication in the Head Hunter's tone. This was why she could never figure out if she disliked him for warranted reasons or not.

Surah stood from her seat, and the three males followed suit. "Thank you for your cooperation," she told the two Hunters.

Then, she turned and left the room, pulling her hood back over her head, the heels of her boots clicking on the hard earth and bouncing off the black walls of the tunnel. Theo followed right at her side.

"What next, my lady?" he asked, and Surah got the impression that he knew exactly what to do next, and was testing her. Seeing if she was up for the job.

She continued down the tunnel that led out of the Mountain, wanting to be free of its suppressing weight, willfully keeping the snap out of her tone. "Now we go see about Merin Nightborn," she said, and Theo smiled as if she were a toddler who'd just recited her ABC's.

The stone that hung around her neck, tucked into her shirt, pulsed against her skin as she thought again about casting a lightning strike at the Head Hunter. Of course, she didn't. There were other matters to attend to, matters that seemed to be growing more imminent by the second.

A Highborn was dead and the Black Stone was missing. It didn't sound like a coincidence to her.

Not at all.

$$4$$

SURAH

The scene of Merin Nightborn's death was just a small bar off the countryside. As soon as Surah saw it, she wondered what a lady like Merin would even have been doing in a place like this—though she had her suspicions, knowing Merin.

Places like this existed solely in the country land; just a small wooden building, not like the trendy bars in the city. The road leading to it and the parking lot were a dusty brown, and two dozen Hunter's griffins were lined up in front. The massive birds eyed me as I passed, their feathers catching the light of the moon and their heads cocking this way and that.

The sign over the bar read *DRINKS*, painted in a fiery red that stood out on the wooden building. Soft light spilled out through the glass door, and the Black Mountain loomed miles in the distance. It was kind of lovely in its simplicity, but Surah felt out of place here immediately in her black cloak and expensive black boots, which caught the dirt on the ground and held it as she walked.

"What could Merin have been doing here?" Surah asked,

more to herself than to anyone else. The sight of the place had made her forget Theo was still at her side.

"That is an excellent question, my lady," Theo said.

Surah took a deep breath of the fresh country air before stepping into the bar, where the aroma would surely be booze and cigarettes. The short heels of her boots clicked on the wooden steps as she climbed up the porch.

Flicking her wrist, the door to the place swung open, and Surah stepped inside.

It wasn't as she had expected, not dirty and dusty, but instead, clean and polished and warm. The lights were set intimately low, the walls a richer, darker wood than the exterior of the building, and paintings of different scenes of the countryside hung on the walls. They were beautifully done oil works, the colors and strokes having captured perfect portraits of the land at optimal moments, as if the artist had sat out all day to wait for the light to fall just right.

Wooden tables with chairs sat in the center of the room, and red booths lined the walls. To the right was the bar, a polished oak that gleamed under the soft lights. Rows of liquor bottles lined the shelves behind it, standing like soldiers, shoulder to glassy shoulder. Surah found herself taking another deep breath, and finding the smell not stale or unpleasant, but clean and inviting, like a grandmother's home.

There were no customers, of course, but Hunters were everywhere, standing around in their black cloaks, moving from here to there, writing things down with their wands. When they saw Surah and Theo, they all stopped what they were doing and bowed to their princess and Head Hunter. Surah waved a hand, telling them to rise. One of the Hunters strode over to them, a tall man with a wiry build and nervous, flicking eyes.

The Hunter bowed again when he reached Surah. "Princess," he said.

"Rise, sir," she said. "Are you the Chief in this jurisdiction?"

The Hunter nodded. "I am, my lady. Hunter Sand. Very pleased to meet you."

"And I you, Sir Sand." Surah looked around at the Hunters, who were looking back at her. "Have your men moved anything?"

Sand shook his head, and Surah could tell he must have just recently been promoted and was uneasy about the job. She thought she could sympathize with that.

"No, my lady. We were waiting for the Keeper."

Surah nodded, choosing to ignore the obvious question on his face asking if that would be her. "Show me, please," she said.

Sand led Theo and Surah over to the bar. The Hunters there parted and lowered their heads respectfully. Her breath caught a little as she saw Merin Nightborn sprawled on the floor, her fine cloak fanned out around her. Her red lips were parted but pulled no air, and her neck was bent at an unnatural angle. Very much dead.

Surah's stomach did not flip or twist at the sight, but something spiraled there. Maybe it was a little intuition, and it told her that this was in no way going to be an open and close case. Something serious was going on in her father's kingdom, and until it was settled she had an obligation to help. For the second time this day, she thought, *Well, shit.*

"Who owns this establishment, Sand?" Theo asked, his eyes going hard at the sight of Lady Nightborn.

"We've got the owner in the back, sitting in his office," said Sand. He paused, that nervousness back in his eyes. "He's got Jude Flyer with him."

Surah raised an eyebrow at that. Jude Flyer was a pretty well known Defender. Not highborn, but very good at what he did, nonetheless. Some of the Highborn Defenders used to laugh at the little male, but that had stopped after he'd won some pretty tough cases. Flyer was uncommonly good at finding evidence that exonerated his clients, even when it looked like they were a step away from the chopping block, their hands all but painted red. The mention of him only made Surah's unease grow.

"Let's see them," Theo said, a smile coming to his handsome face that Surah didn't like one bit.

Theo allowed Surah to go first, as was the custom. She flicked her wrist, using a bit of magic so that the door to the small office behind the bar swung open. Then she stepped inside.

And paused in her tracks.

She couldn't say how she knew it was him, just that she knew. He still looked the same as in her memory, even though he had grown older, of course. He had gone from a boy to a man, his body having filled out and grown hard with what she knew had to be years of actual labor. Not the cultivated muscles that Theo wore, but harder somehow, as though they had been earned through callouses and sweat. Dark hair had grown in across his strong jawline, and his eyes were still the emerald of tropical ocean water that Surah remembered so clearly. He wore only a flannel shirt, faded jeans, and work boots on his feet. His position was relaxed, reclined in the chair behind the desk, fingers laced together over his chest, as though he had been sitting right there for hours.

Surah pulled her eyes away from him and they settled on Jude Flyer, who also looked as though he'd been sitting a while. He ran a hand through his thin, slicked-back hair and rose from his chair. After a moment, as though he had momentarily forgotten his manners, his client did the same.

Both men bowed to their princess.

"Princess," Jude said, offering a chubby-fingered hand. Surah sighed mentally as she held her own out to be kissed, glad once more that she always wore her gloves, especially since it was the same hand Jude had run through his greasy hair. "It is an honor," continued the Defender.

Surah smiled tightly and nodded. She pulled her hand from his and took a seat in one of the two chairs opposite the desk, all too aware that the other male's eyes followed her the whole time. Surah glanced over at him to see the smallest change of expression cross his face, a slight movement that made her cock her head just a fraction.

From behind her, Theo said, "Good evening," and Surah thought maybe Charlie's expression had shifted—only momentarily, his face was back to blank already—because of the Head Hunter.

Charlie.

That was his name. She remembered now. Just like that. *Charlie Redmine.* A good, simple name. She rolled it around in her head a little, thinking maybe rolling it off her tongue would be pleasant as well. It was hard to equate him with the boy from her memories. He had grown into such a...*man.*

She slapped those thoughts away. Those thoughts were no good. Those thoughts were futile.

Theo took a seat beside her, and Surah wished very much for no reason at all that the Head Hunter were not here with her, that she could do this on her own, even though she didn't even entirely know *what* she was doing. Surah's job in her father's kingdom over the past ten years had involved two things; helping the king make diplomatic decisions, and looking pretty and proper for the public. Most people just thought she did the latter, but many of the laws and assistance programs her father had passed over time were of Surah's creation, and the public was glad for them. She'd never cared about getting credit for the work. She was just glad to be giving back.

But being a Keeper and being a politician were two different things. Work that involved hands-on action, not just power of the mind.

"What happened here?" Theo said, his words clipped. Surah restrained herself from shifting uneasily.

Jude Flyer answered, "Mr. Redmine was in the process of closing this establishment tonight when Lady Nightborn arrived. She sat at the bar, ordered a drink. About five minutes later, a Demon entered and attacked. It killed Lady Nightborn and fled."

The Head Hunter's eyes were locked on Charlie, and Surah had to stop herself from shifting uncomfortably again, though she had no idea why.

"Is that so, *Charlie*?" Theo asked, making the name sound like a dirty thing.

Charlie nodded, his emerald eyes holding the Head Hunter's steadily, without fear. "Yes," he said. "It happened fast. I tried to help her, but the Demon seemed to be on a mission. There was nothing I could do."

"Why would a Demon be here in the middle of nowhere?'" The incredulity was as thick as molasses in Theo's tone.

"That's a good question," Charlie said.

Surah found herself staring at Charlie's lips, listening to the way the country land rode his words. It was so unlike the High-speech she was used to, almost exotic. And then she pulled her eyes away and stopped those thoughts again. No good, those were. She needed to focus.

"You realize," Theo said, "that you are the only witness to the death of a Highborn lady. You expect us to believe you?"

Charlie shrugged, still holding the Head Hunter's gaze. "I can't explain it," he said. "I thought that was your job. I'm just telling you what happened."

Surah stiffened. The whole room seemed to stiffen. She couldn't blame Charlie for saying this. Theo's very tone was accusatory, but it took balls to talk to the Head Hunter in that way. Really big balls, especially from a commoner, and Surah found herself admiring Charlie Redmine's courage and wishing he would shut up at the same time.

"We very much intend to explain it," Theo said, his words clipped. "That's *exactly* what we intend to do."

Surah removed the glove from her right hand, wanting to stop this conversation for reasons she didn't really understand. She leaned forward and placed her hand on the desk, palm up. Looking straight at Charlie, her heart picked up a little in pace. She cursed it for doing so, and willed it to stop its girlish yammering.

"Would you mind repeating the story for me, Mr. Redmine?" she asked, her sweet voice the exact opposite of Theo's tone.

Charlie's eyes met hers, and Surah felt something warm spiral in her stomach. She bit her tongue to try and force it away. His eyes seemed to really *look* at her, to almost *burn* through her, and she wondered if all women found his gaze so penetrating or if her hormones were just getting the best of her. This made her think of Lady Nightborn, and suddenly, Surah thought she might have an explanation for what Merin had been doing here. This made a terrible feeling of dread spiral in Surah's stomach.

Charlie's large hand came up and rested in hers, his palm rough and warm, his fingers engulfing hers. Her heart jumped again, and she told it sternly that that was quite enough out of it. She needed to concentrate.

"Whenever you're ready, Mr. Redmine" she said, and swallowed when Charlie just sat staring at her.

She could feel rather than see Theo beside her. She didn't like it.

"It's just like Mr. Flyer said," Charlie began, "Lady Nightborn came in and ordered a drink around closing time. The Demon came after. I've never seen anything like it. Its eyes were glowing red. It slipped in so fast, broke Merin's neck and left."

"Merin?" scoffed the Head Hunter. "Are you so familiar, Mr. Redmine?"

Charlie said nothing to this.

Surah suppressed a sigh. "He's telling the truth, Hunter Gray," she said, releasing Charlie's hand.

This clearly did not please Theo. His gray eyes seemed to go a shade darker, and his mouth pressed into a thin line.

"Demons need to be summoned," Theo said. "What other reason would it have to be here?"

Charlie shrugged. "I told you, I don't know."

Theo smiled, but it was too toothy to be anything but a threat. Charlie only stared back in defiance.

"Well, you were right about one thing, Mr. Redmine," the Head Hunter said, "it is my job to get to the bottom of this, and I can promise you that I will."

5

———

SURAH

Surah paced back and forth across the ancient Arkian rug that covered her bedroom floor.

Samson watched her from his perch by the window, his enormous head resting between his paws, his ears perked and long tail tucked around him. He had been chuffing and sniffing around her since she entered, but now, he just watched her, his golden tiger-eyes following her back and forth.

"Dear Gods, Samson," she said, going over to him and running her hand through the soft fur on his neck. "What is going on here?"

Samson was a Great Tiger, about four times the size of those in the human world, his stripes blue and black rather than orange and black. Surah had saved him from a Great Serpent when he had been just a cub, and the beast was loyal to her beyond all else.

Her father's eyes had bugged out of his head when Surah had walked home with Samson one evening when she was just a girl, some fifteen years ago, and she had cried and cried until he finally agreed to let the tiger stay. It was impossible not to see how the tiger loved her, and eventually Syrian decided the beast would be good protection for his daughter.

"I need to think," Surah whispered, wrapping her arms around Samson's neck and nuzzling her face against his warm, thick fur. Samson let out a deep purr and licked his mistress's face with his rough tongue. He spoke in her head, an ability Surah had given him using magic long ago. She was the only one who communicated with him this way, because he simply didn't care to communicate with anyone else.

His voice was deep and rumbling. *"Is he the boy you saved all those years ago?"*

"Yes," she silently responded.

"And you believe he's innocent?" Samson said.

"He wasn't lying about what happened with Merin... but he may have been withholding something."

Samson licked her hand to comfort her, and she rubbed his huge head as she thought. The tiger's eyes closed and he leaned into her hand. She was going to have to solve this problem, and the faster the better. She was a pragmatic person by nature, and made more so by time. She needed two things; to find the Black Stone, and to find the truth about Merin Nightborn's death. She was locked now into the position of Keeper for the time being, and she needed to do her job well.

Surah brought her right hand up, holding her fingers together as if clutching a pencil, and began to write in the air. The piece of White Stone tucked into her shirt grew warm against her chest. The words hung before her eyes on an invisible sheet of paper, but Surah was the only one who could see them. It was a simple kind of magic, like a mental filing system, much less risky than writing things down in a journal or with a wand, as common folks did, but most people never took the time to learn it. Her brother Syris had taught her this, had told her it was an important skill to have, and now she could really see why. She had to put the puzzle pieces together.

This was what she knew: The Black Stone was missing. Merin Nightborn was dead. The only witness to the deaths was a man who she'd met once as a girl. He was the boy she'd helped escape Theodine's clutches after he'd been caught stealing, and Surah had received a moon cycle of punishment for helping him.

Now, he was the main suspect in Merin's death by sheer proximity. And if Demons were involved, as he had claimed, then someone was brewing something. Something big.

Charlie Redmine. She wondered how she could have forgotten his name. .

Surah sighed and stood, patting Samson on the head absent-mindedly. The morning sun was just beginning to brighten the sky, filling the horizon with soft blues and pinks. She probably should have tried to get some sleep, but it was too late for that now. The next step was going to see her father, and she wondered what her report would be. Should she mention her brief history with Charlie? Did it even matter? She didn't know the man from Adam. She certainly didn't owe him anything.

A moment later she was sweeping into her father's study, where Syrian sat in his chair in front of the fire. A table had been set up in front of him, and a breakfast of exotic fruits and meats and fresh bread was sprawled out there. He looked over at his daughter as she entered and smiled around a mouthful of food.

"Surah," he said, "how were your travels?"

Surah took a seat in the chair across from her father, staring into the fireplace as if the answers to her questions burned there. She folded her gloved hands in her lap, her heart seeming to sink down into the chair with her.

"Travels were fine, father," she said.

Syrian was silent for a moment. "Are you hungry?" he asked.

Surah gave her father a smile and nodded. The two of them could fight like cats and dogs, but they had an overall good relationship. They took care of each other. They loved each other, and they were the only immediate family either of them had left.

Silence hung between them, Syrian waiting patiently for Surah to speak, as he knew was best with her. A servant entered the room and delivered a tray of food for her that matched her father's. The two of them sat eating for a time. Then, Surah finally decided to just jump in.

"It doesn't look good, father," she said, fixing her purple gaze on him.

Syrian's square jaw worked as he chewed, his face settling into that of a king doing business. Again, he waited for her to speak.

Surah told the story, leaving out the history with Charlie. For now.

When she was finished, Syrian sat back and released a slow breath, folding his large hands on his ample belly over the silver chain resting there that held his piece of White Stone, which was twice the size of hers. Surah knew what his first question would be.

"Was he lying?"

Yep. First question. Sometimes she hated that her father was so in-tuned to her. No one in the world could read her like him now that Syris was dead. She was careful not to avert her eyes. She hadn't known before if she would tell him the truth, but like always, she found it difficult to lie to him.

"I don't think the witness is guilty of murdering Merin Nightborn, or of stealing the Black Stone," she said. "It's…complicated."

Syrian raised an eyebrow at this. "Oh, I would say so, Surah. I would indeed say so. But my question is, why do *you* think it's complicated?"

Surah sat back and sighed. "Well, the Black Stone is missing and Lady Nightborn was indeed murdered," Surah began. "The only witness claimed it was a Demon who came in and broke her neck… The question is, how are these things connected? Or are they connected at all?"

Syrian said nothing, only waited.

Now for the bombshell. Surah breathed deep. "I just don't believe Charlie Redmine has anything to do with the missing stone, or the murder because—"

"What was that name?" Syrian snapped, cutting her off before she could finish. His face had gone hard, his mouth tight and fingers digging into the armrests of his chair. Surah's heart dropped, and she hadn't even known it'd been at risk of falling.

"Charlie Redmine?" she said, her voice just above a whisper. She didn't like the look on her father's face.

Syrian spoke through clenched teeth. "I thought I remembered it from somewhere. Is Redmine still in custody?"

Surah swallowed, nodded. The blazing fireplace suddenly seemed very hot at her side.

Her father seemed to relax a little. "Good. Have him locked up immediately pending investigation," he said. Now his violet gaze fixed on her.

"Who is he, father? How do you know him?"

Syrian stared at her, and Surah's breath seemed to freeze in her chest. Whatever he was about to tell her, she probably didn't want to hear it. Just by his look she could tell it was going to seriously complicate matters.

"He's Black Heart's younger brother," Syrian said.

Surah wasn't sure why, but for a moment, she couldn't breathe at all.

6

SURAH

*A*s soon as she did it, she wished she hadn't.

In one hour Hunters would be here to haul Charlie Redmine to the cells, and she would be leading the arrest. Now, she stood in his living room, having just opened a portal from her chambers. She'd told her father she would report back to Theo and have him ready a team to arrest Charlie, but she'd come here instead.

She saw him first. He sat asleep on the couch, an old wooden guitar perched on his lap, his handsome face peaceful, instead of scowling for once. Surah tore her eyes away and glanced around nervously, taking his slumber as a sign from the Gods that she better just leave now before it was too late.

She was just about to snap her fingers and get the hell out of there when she stole one last look at the sleeping man to see that he was no longer sleeping.

His emerald eyes were open, staring at her in that penetrating way they had. Her fingers relaxed and her hand fell to her side, thoughts of leaving momentarily forgotten. Charlie said nothing, just sat up a little, straitening his flannel shirt, and slowly placed the guitar on the floor, his gaze never leaving Surah's.

She froze. Couldn't think of a single thing to say. His face was carefully expressionless.

"Princess," he said.

This snapped Surah out of her trance. "You're going to be arrested," she said, deciding to cut to the chase. The longer she stayed here, the worse it could be. For both of them.

Charlie's shoulders tightened, his eyes narrowing a fraction.

"Is your brother Black Heart?" she asked.

Charlie's face was carefully blank. "Yes."

Surah waited for elaboration.

"I haven't spoken to him in years," Charlie said after a moment.

Surah moved away from him, turning her back on his piercing gaze, and went over to the wall where more paintings like the ones in his bar hung.

She looked over her shoulder at him. "Did you do these?" she asked, gesturing to the paintings.

Charlie nodded.

"They're beautiful," she said, wondering why in the hell she was making small talk with the clock ticking the way it was. She was not at all sure she could trust him, or even why she was here in the first place.

"Thank you,," Charlie said, his deep, country-accented voice low and wary.

This place was so different from the way Surah lived, so simple and cozy, and it fascinated her. She wondered if all the common people in the country land lived so simply.

"You should cooperate," she said turning to face him again. "If you really had nothing to do with Lady Nightborn's death, and you're innocent in all this, you have nothing to worry about."

Charlie snorted. "Yeah, right," he said. "We're not all heir to the throne, princess. That's not how things work."

Surah was taken aback by his flippant tone, but wasn't sure what else she should expect from him. He'd told her when they were children that he hated Highborns, and from the way his lips twisted when he looked at Theo and the other Hunters, he hadn't much changed his mind since then.

As usual, Surah opted for being diplomatic. "I'm the Keeper for the time being, which makes me the head of the investigation. If you're innocent, I should be able to prove it."

Charlie's head tilted, and he stood, unfolding his muscular body from the couch. He didn't approach her, but there was only a couple of feet of space between them, and Surah felt her heartbeat kick up a touch.

After studying her a moment, he walked over to the fireplace with lithe movements.

Without looking back at her, he said, "And if you can't prove it, princess? Then, what? What happens to a common Sorcerer who's convicted of killing a Highborn?"

Surah knew that the question was rhetorical; they both knew the answer good and well.

"You'll just have to trust me, I guess," she said, and the words sounded lame even to her own ears.

When Charlie looked at her now, her breath caught in her throat. Those deep green eyes held hers with the same defiant fire that had burned there when he'd been younger.

He gave her a smirk as handsome as a devil's, but there was no humor behind it.

"You're not the one I don't trust, princess," he said.

WHEN SURAH RETURNED LESS than an hour later with Theo and two other Hunters, Charlie gave no indication that he had seen her just before.

Her stomach was in knots, because she was almost sure that rather than taking her advice and cooperating, Charlie would run, and then as Keeper, she would be forced to chase him, which would in turn damage his case for innocence.

But Charlie Redmine had not run. Instead, he only sneered at the Hunters and allowed them to put magical cuffs around his wrists.

As Theo opened a portal into the dungeons beneath the castle in Zadira and shoved Charlie into the cold, dank cell, Surah second-guessed her advice to him.

Perhaps he should have run.

The look in Charlie's deep green eyes said he was thinking the exact same thing.

7

———

SURAH

*S*amson walked alongside her as Surah crossed the courtyard separating her father's quarters and her own. She could have just opened a portal into the foyer outside of his office, but she needed the time to think.

Her tiger walked closely at her flank, his enormous head lowered, amber eyes seeing everything they passed, ears perked and tail swishing slowly. A large stone wall with hundreds of tiny waterfalls was to the left, and the other three walls crawled with green vines that sprouted thousands of violet flowers with blood-red centers.

The sky above was open for all to see, blue with puffs of white cloud drifting across, the air carrying a sweet floral scent. Hunters and lords, ladies, and visiting dignitaries met here, sipping caffeinated drinks and discussing political matters on the pathways and lawns, the benches and fountains. It was a lovely place, but Surah avoided places like these. Too populated.

They all bowed as she passed by, and she nodded and princess-smiled as was her duty, wondering if any of them were aware of Merin Nightborn's death, thinking the answer was probably no. Not yet, at least. She was beyond grateful for this, but the peace wouldn't keep for long. Soon, everyone would know, and being Keeper, they would look to her for justice.

Samson watched them all, and she knew that he could smell the small tang of fear that radiated from them as he moved by. He was not a tame beast, but he had been at Surah's side for centuries, and had learned how to control himself. For her.

The tiger's head turned sharply as Theodine Gray fell into step on the other side of Surah. Surah offered a friendly nod, but wished like hell he would just go away. Theo seemed to be buzzing around like a fly lately, and the urge to swat at him was getting stronger and stronger.

"My lady," Theo said.

So much for time to think. She may as well have just travelled by portal. "Sir Gray," she said.

"On your way to see King Syrian?" he asked.

Surah nodded, reaching over to stroke Samson's side for comfort. She could feel the powerful muscles moving in his shoulders as he walked.

They reached the wall that held the entrance to her father's quarters, and two Hunters stepped aside to let them enter. Theo flicked his wrist, magic swirling around his fingers, and the doors swung open for them. They stepped into the foyer with the storm mural hanging above, and two more Hunters bowed to them in greeting.

Theo came to a stop at the center of the room, halting Surah's progress as well. They were alone here, save for the four Hunters that always occupied the space, as silent as the candelabras hanging on the walls. Surah looked up at the Head Hunter, her eyebrow cocked, her heart sinking a little for a reason she couldn't explain after seeing the look on his face.

"May I have a word with you, princess?" Theo asked.

Surah swallowed. *No,* she thought, *please don't.*

She nodded.

Theo rubbed his hands together, his handsome face apprehensive. It took Surah a moment to recognize that he was nervous, as she couldn't recall a time ever seeing him so. She found herself holding her breath.

"I would hope," Theo began, just barely above a whisper, "that you know how I feel about you." His gloved hands came up and took hers, and Surah had to use great effort not to take a step back. His gray eyes were all but burning. "I have loved you since we were children, Surah," he admitted.

Theo paused, his handsome face dead serious, his jaw tight, watching for how she absorbed this information. Surah just looked at him, not sure what to say to this. The urge to hop on Samson's back and let him carry her out of there like she used to do when she was a little girl struck her, and she bit her tongue to keep back the laugh that mental image brought up.

"And I hope," Theo continued, "that you will consider accepting my hand in marriage."

At these words Surah's thoughts seemed to jam up, and she could not think of what to say. Of course, she did not want to marry Theodine Gray, but that didn't mean she wanted to break his heart in front of four of his Hunters. She had to concentrate not to shift on her feet, as the situation was inherently uncomfortable.

Then a thought came, and it was only one word, a name actually, but it was as clear as Kadari crystal.

Charlie.

Her brow furrowed. Why was she thinking of Charlie? That was no good. She shoved the thought away, opening her mouth to say something, not knowing what it would be until it came out.

"You'll have to give me time to consider things," she said, and cleared her throat as the solution came to her, her voice adopting the confidence that always carried in her sweet tone. "There is much to be done now, too much that requires my attention."

Theo's expression changed, not so much a hardening, as she was used to seeing from him, but more a poker mask sliding into place. Surah felt a pang of guilt. She had never seen this expression on Theo's face, and it was strangely disarming. She thought for just a moment that if he always wore this look, rather than the smug one he put on for all others, she might not dislike him so much. Her gloved hand reached up before she could stop it.

It rested against Theo's face, and his eyes softened as he leaned his chin into her touch. For a moment Surah could see why so many women were in love with him, and she had to work a little to hold his gaze. She gave him her gentlest princess smile, and he didn't know the difference. So few would.

"I will consider it, Theo," she said, "and I am honored that you have asked." She swallowed. "But there are other matters at hand…you understand?" Her voice was sweet and low, the purr of a kitten. One of her more deceptive qualities.

Theo smiled, flashing perfect teeth. He really was a handsome man, with fine lines to his face and dark lashes. He took Surah's hand into his and kissed it, bowing his head.

"Of course, my lady," he said.

Surah was just breathing a sigh of relief when something nudged her hard in the back, making her stumble forward into Theo's arms. He caught her quickly and set her to rights, and Surah whipped her head around to see Samson staring at her, his amber eyes only inches from her own, his huge chest puffing as he chuffed and growled deeply. He sent her one word telepathically, then he shot off across the foyer in the direction of the king's quarters.

The one word was *trouble*.

Surah didn't think twice. She took to her heels and chased her tiger down the hallway to her father's study, her heart beating out of her chest, the stone at her throat growing alternately hot and cold. Samson had heard something. Something was wrong. She could feel it too now. *Big* trouble.

The tiger slammed head-first into the double doors to the study, crashing them open with cracks like thunder, and charged into the room. Surah followed only moments after, with Theo right at her heels.

Her breath caught in her throat as she took in the scene. Her father stood off to the side, his thick hands raised and moving through the air in ceaseless motion as his lips recited spell after spell after spell. Lightning flew from his fingertips like snakes of silver. His face was all concentrated, sharp lines, and his hair stood up on end as if electricity were passing through him.

Magic was so thick in here that it floated on the air like smoke and charged the room with heat like a divine furnace. King Syrian's two personal Hunters lay dead on the floor. Blood ran down the walls, pooled on the soft purple carpet. The screeches and screams of the damned bounced off the walls and floor and ceiling. The enormous fireplace in the west wall blazed like the infernos of hell.

And out of it poured demons.

Surah rolled her neck and removed the two sais that she always kept crisscrossed at her back, thinking this was turning out to be one hell of a day.

8

SURAH

Samson charged forward, his muscular body held low and his amber eyes flashing with battle lust. He leapt into the air and clamped his huge jaws around the black, rotted body of a demon, snatching it out of flight like a dazed fly.

The Demon shrieked, its cry of agony ripping through Surah's ears as the tiger and the thing came crashing to the ground, Samson's teeth ripping at the black skeletal figure and sending oily blood and body parts in all directions.

The smell in the room was awful, like that of death. Nearly choking.

Another demon swept down toward Surah, skeletal black wings blowing the heat of the fireplace against her face, lifting her short lavender hair from her shoulders. Her heart leapt as she spun around with her sais and skewered the thing right through the midsection, its long claws reaching and scraping, its red eyes widening and mouth gaping. Her lips trembled as she uttered a banishing spell. The thing disappeared in a thick cloud of black smoke, leaving behind only the smell of burning flesh and spoiled fruit.

For a short moment that seemed incredibly long, all she

could do was stand there and stare around the room. She had seen a demon or two before, but she had never seen *so many* demons before. The sight was nearly paralyzing. Like watching a scene in hell.

It reminded her of the battle she'd witnessed a month ago in a place called the Silver City run by the Vampires and Wolves. In all her life she had never seen such a thing as she had that night, and she still wished she never had. She had watched the young Sun Warrior charge into battle, could still see so clearly the deep red that spilled into the stark white snow, the steamy breath that issued from the mouths of so many dying, visible last moments of life. She remembered the moment when the young Warrior lost her mind, the battle lust overcoming her and the destruction that followed. The look in the girl's eyes—Alexa, her name was Alexa—was the same look that now rode behind the glowing red eyes of the demons in the room. The eyes were dark abysses. You stared into them, and they stared back.

And the smell. That awful, awful smell.

It was nearly paralyzing indeed, but when another demon whipped its head toward her, fiery eyes flashing and sharp claws raised, its throat issuing that ear-clenching screech, she snapped out of her reverie and slid into battle mode.

It was not difficult. Death was the only thing in life Surah knew to be a certainty, and as much as she had faced it, she also dealt it when necessary. If not for the worry for her father, who was currently fighting off a demon of his own, and moving not quite as fast as he used to, she thought she might enjoy this. Battling demons was not something one got the opportunity to do often.

She gripped her weapons, the ends of which were black with rotted blood, dripping ropes of it. Her cloak fluttered with her movements, dancing around her as she moved through the room and battled the demons like an angel dancing on storm clouds.

Beside her, Theodine Gray danced with his sword as well, and slid its blade across the throat of another demon, its shrieks of anger and agony filling the room.

But Syrian was moving too slowly. Just her glimpses of him —his movement stiff, his eyes bulging and the vein in his forehead standing out—told her they were in serious trouble here. They were too far outnumbered.

And more were coming out of the hearth. Ugly, black creatures with glowing red eyes, their bodies nothing but bone and rotted muscle. Their hands were claws and their feet hooves. Horns protruded from their skulls, beneath which sat faces from nightmares. Bat-like wings flapped at their backs, stirring the hot air and pushing the scent of decay and death around the room in rank waves. Surah had to close the portal they were coming through, or at least try. Gods only knew how long they could hold the demons off.

"Samson," she said, her voice sounding strange in the unintelligible chaos of the room. Small somehow. Out of place.

The tiger's huge head whipped toward her. He moved to her side immediately, leaping into the air again and severing the body of a demon with his powerful jaws in mid-flight. He landed on his paws in front of her, black blood marring his fur and teeth, and shook his head, whipping a piece of rotted demon flesh against the wall, where it splattered like a bug and slid down to the floor in a nasty pool.

Surah clutched the stone at her throat and closed her eyes, knowing Samson would protect her while she did this. She ran through the spell Syris had taught her for closing portals to deeper dimensions, hoping she would get it right. She had only ever performed it once in training with her brother, and he'd had to help a good deal.

She recited the words, her brow furrowing in concentration,

doing her best to ignore the growls of her tiger and the cries of the damned, the pure *wrongness* in the room.

Sweat trickled down her back as she clenched her hands into fists and recited faster, the stone squeezed in the palm of her hand burning now. Her head grew light with the effort, the power washing through her and sweeping her away. She planted her feet and continued, her breath coming short and heart pounding like a death toll.

She felt it when it worked, like a puzzle piece snapping into place, and all sound seemed momentarily sucked out of the room. The wonderful feeling that accompanied successful magic swept through her, and her eyes snapped open and propelled her back to the scene. She looked first to the stone fireplace, and breathed a huge breath as no more demons came out of it.

A screech issued to her left, where Theo was removing the head of one of the remaining demons, his left hand gripping the demon's large horn as he ran his blade across the thing's throat, his lips moving swiftly in a banishing spell, the small Head Hunter's stone around his neck glowing red.

Then, she looked to her right, where her father was sending two more demons away in noxious clouds of black smoke, his big chest heaving in a way that made more worry spiral in Surah's stomach.

Samson sat at her side, licking black blood from his paws and teeth, his eyes narrowed to slits and powerful shoulders relaxed, as though he'd just finished dinner rather than killing demons.

At last, it was done.

Four Hunters came rushing through the double doors of the study, way too late to the party, and stood staring at the scene in the room with slightly wide eyes, the only indication of their alarm.

Surah looked down at herself, eyeing the rank black demon

blood marring her cloak and gloves. She felt a trickle of something roll down her neck and reached up to wipe at it, suppressing a gag when she saw that it was more of the nasty blood.

She ran her hands down the air in front of her, reciting a spell to clean away the mess, and drew a few deep breaths after she'd set herself to rights. Her father and Theo cleaned themselves off as well, and the three stood looking at each other not knowing at all what to say.

It was Theo who broke the silence. He slid his sword into the back of his cloak and his jaw clenched. "I better go check on the prisoner," he said.

9

SURAH

*S*urah followed on Theo's heels, not wanting to give him a chance to abuse Charlie, but when they got there, she stopped in her tracks, her blood going cold.

Standing in the cell with Charlie was a Sorcerer she would know anywhere, so notorious he was for his actions in her father's kingdom.

Black Heart.

And also Charlie's brother, reminded a small voice in her head.

Surah only had time to meet Charlie's gaze once before the two Sorcerers disappeared from the cell, somehow opening a portal despite the magic in place that was supposed to prevent that.

Her heart didn't sink. She didn't know him well enough for her heart to sink, but it tilted. She examined the emotion as they stood there in silence, staring at the spot where Charlie Redmine and Black Heart had been just a moment ago. It was just a beat of time, but in it she acknowledged that she felt a little disappointed at this new development, at what she'd just seen. It was then she realized she'd really wanted Charlie to be innocent, to come out of this unscathed.

But the moment passed on a single bated breath, and she wiped the thoughts away as one might chalk from a blackboard. Why should she be disappointed? They had only met once before, when they had just barely been teenagers, and she had been a stupid young girl.

Theo broke the silence, which he seemed to be doing a lot lately. His voice was hard and deep. "Can you perform a tracking spell, my lady?" he asked.

Surah nodded, her head curiously light on her shoulders. She kept trying to shove thoughts of Charlie away, and found the name kept coming back, along with the tropical ocean color of his eyes, the calmness and control that radiated from them. His eyes were the only things that were the same as she remembered, but she couldn't remember having this reaction to him before.

Surely she was too wise to be as vain as to be spellbound by just his appearance, though she had to admit said appearance had become rather spellbinding. There was no denying that; he was a good-looking man. A very good-looking man. But so what? If you asked most people, so was Theodine Gray. It meant nothing. Or at least, it shouldn't.

"How long will it take you to prepare?" Theo asked yanking her out of her troublesome thoughts.

Surah's mouth felt a little dry. She licked her lips. "Half an hour," she said, "and I'll need to consult with Bassil first."

Theo nodded and opened the door that led out into the hallway. Surah stepped through, and he followed, shutting the door behind him. "I'll have the Warlock sent to your quarters."

Surah forced herself to look up into Theo's gray eyes and smile. She may not be too fond of him, but at least he wasn't a liar. She refused to recognize the twist of her stomach that came with that thought.

"Thank you," she said.

Then she snapped her fingers and opened a portal back to

her chambers to prepare the spell that might track down Charlie Redmine and his brother.

She couldn't say for certain if she hoped it would work or not.

* * *

Bottles clanked together and flew from the shelf inside the cabinet, floating on the air and settling on the counter in a neat row.

Surah walked in front of them and read the labels, her posture stiff and rigid, placing the ones she needed in a pile off to the side without even touching them. Her father would have thought it a useless application of magic, but Surah was on edge, and she didn't particularly care what her father would say right now. He'd forced this work on her, shoving her into being Keeper, and she would complete the tasks in the manner she pleased, because backing out now was not an option.

Bassil stood behind her, motionless, watching. His hands were tucked into the sleeves of his cloak where he crossed his huge arms over his chest. Surah turned her head to the side, looking up at him from the corner of her eye.

"Quit staring at me like that, Bassil." She smiled a little. "It's creepy."

Bassil chuckled, a deep, rich laugh that matched the dark tone of his skin. His white teeth glinted behind a wide smile. His voice was slightly accented by the Northlands, even after all these years. He turned on his heel, making his multi-colored, patchwork cloak flip around his legs, and went over to the window to sit by Samson.

The Warlock patted the tiger between the ears. Samson lay unmoving, his huge head resting on his paws, amber eyes watching his mistress. He didn't lean into the touch. He would let Bassil and a select few others pet him, but he only responded to Surah's hands.

"As you wish, princess," Bassil said. "You just go on and keep flinging bottles off the shelf like a worried Elf's wife."

Surah spun around on her heels, the smile gone from her face, her voice flat, her princess-etiquette momentarily discarded.

"The Black Stone is missing, Warlock. A Highborn lady is dead. Demons just flew out of my father's fireplace and tried to kill him. How is it you think I should be acting?"

Bassil clasped his hands together in front of him and smiled humbly. "Ah, a real reaction from the princess. You are getting better at showing your emotions, my lady."

Surah's head tilted back, a mischievous glint in her eye, and she flung a bottle of purple potion at the Warlock with her magic. Bassil laughed and his hand shot up, halting the bottle mid-flight. He moved his hand to the side and the vial settled on Surah's dresser. Surah relaxed a little, taking comfort in the interaction. She had grown up with Bassil. He had been her mentor since she was a little girl, and this was a normal exchange between them.

"You still throw like a princess, I see," he said.

Surah rolled her eyes and continued picking out bottles for the spell.

"I thought you were here to help me," she said. "Isn't there something you should be setting up? What do we pay you for?"

Bassil laughed again. "My wise council, of course, and you seem to be doing a fair job of it yourself, my lady."

Surah inventoried her selections so far, turning her back to Bassil and replacing the unneeded bottles. "Maybe I should tell Samson to bite you," she said.

Bassil looked down to see the tiger looking at him with those golden eyes, and took a step away from the window where Samson was perched. He knew Surah wasn't serious, but the tiger had been listening, and now he could practically see the idea playing out in the beast's head.

"Very funny, my lady," he said.

Surah smiled and gathered the bottles, moving over to the table by the window and placing them on top before taking a seat in the chair there. Bassil claimed the seat across from her, eyeing the ingredients.

"This would work better with eagle's blood," he said.

Surah's purple eyes lifted to the Warlock's face, her hands pausing over the small bowl she was arranging at the center of the table.

"Perhaps," she said, "but that's black magic. You know this, Bassil."

The Warlock nodded once. "True, but you're *searching* for darkness. It lays on the horizon, princess, rolling toward the land as we speak. Black magic killed Merin Nightborn and allowed demons to enter your father's chamber. Black magic may be the only way to face the things ahead."

Surah's teeth clenched. A terribly cold shiver walked up her spine. Bassil's voice had taken on that haunting tone she'd learned to both trust and fear over the years. She gave him a level stare, restraining a reaction that would give away her unease, retaining her manners.

"I'll try this way first," she said.

The Warlock spread his hands. "Of course, my lady."

She spent the next thirty minutes attempting the spell, staring into the mixture of potions in the bowl, concentrating until sweat rolled down her neck, saying the incantations over and over again, until finally, she sat back and blew out a heavy breath. She brought her gloved hands up and rubbed her forehead, squeezing her eyes shut.

Bassil raised an eyebrow. "No luck?"

Surah opened her eyes and gave him an annoyed look.

The Warlock smiled. "I see."

Just then, there was a knock at the door to her room. Silence fell over them as they stared at each other, unmoving. A second knock sounded, and Surah dragged her eyes over to the door. Samson had lifted his head from his paws, his ears swiveling and perking. Surah took a deep breath and flicked her wrist, opening the door with her magic.

Theodine Gray stood there. Of course he did.

His appearances were routine lately. And by the look on his face Surah could tell he did not have good news to share. Why would he? Things were on that kind of track lately, and she knew from experience that bad times had a way of proceeding worse, like sliding down a slope slicked with oil.

Or blood.

She felt the truth of the Warlock's prediction in that moment, all the way down to her bones, as the Head Hunter delivered the word.

Another Highborn woman was dead.

Yes, darkness was indeed coming, rolling in like storm clouds.

10

SURAH

Surah patted Samson's head before entering the Grand Room, where she knew dozens of royals would be waiting. The tiger leaned into her touch, his amber eyes sympathetic.

"Remember," he told her silently, *"don't mention the Black Stone. Your father doesn't want them to panic."* He paused. *"I don't want them to panic, either. It makes them smell like lunch."*

Surah nodded once, gave her tiger a quick hug, and took a deep breath. She squared her shoulders and tilted up her chin, slipping on the royal posture and mask that she'd learned from her mother as a child.

This was certain to be an unpleasant experience, but in her life she'd dealt with thousands of those, and her mother always said that composure was key. Surah agreed. She rolled her neck and went into the room, Samson at her heels.

As soon as she entered, dozens of faces turned toward her and conversation stopped. The lords and ladies bowed to her, and Surah nodded to them, her heart twisting to see that many of them had tears streaked down their faces.

Merin Nightborn's family stood off to the side in a cluster, mother and father clutching each other, cloaks all black to represent their mourning.

Everyone in the room was wearing black, actually, and for a moment Surah's mind flashed back to the demons that had flown out of her father's fireplace, with their shrieks of anger and agony and their dead, rotted faces.

King Syrian sat at the head of the room on his throne, an enormous thing made of metal and polished wood the color of violet, where a similarly violet runner led up to his feet over the marble floor.

Around him stood his two new personal guards, since his previous ones had died in the demon attack, which was another thing Surah was not supposed to mention. She walked gracefully up to her father's side, taking the hands of those she passed and offering condolences to those who had lost someone in a sort of macabre mingle.

Merin Nightborn's mother had smeared mascara under her puffy red eyes, and her hands shook as she kissed the back of Surah's. Surah pulled her into a hug and held her for a moment, earning a collective sigh from the room.

This was why she was so loved in the kingdom, and she knew it. Not because she went around smiling and greeting her people, but because she actually cared when they were hurting, and she hurt with them. Maybe even more so than her father.

And, now, they would turn to her not just for comfort, but also for answers and justice. Her respect for her lost brother grew in that moment. Being Keeper was not a pleasant job.

When she reached the head of the room she turned and faced her people, bowing to her father as she stood beside his throne, waiting for him to start the dialogue, but someone in the crowd spoke first.

It was Merin Nightborn's father.

"My Liege," he said. "What is being done about my daughter?" His voice broke on that last word, and Surah's chest tightened. She'd just lost her own brother last month, and she understood his heartache. She understood it too well.

King Syrian spoke gently, his composure as solid as Surah's, though she knew he didn't like any of this just as much as she didn't.

"We are doing everything we can to bring light to the situation regarding Merin's untimely death, Lord Nightborn," he said. "And we will bring to justice those responsible."

Gregert Lancer spoke next, his voice as unsteady as Lord Nightborn's. He was the father of Cynthian Lancer, the second Highborn lady who had been killed in the past two days.

A death a day. No wonder the tension in the room was thick. If this kept up, if Surah couldn't find a way to stop it, soon the whole kingdom would be crying out for answers and justice.

In fact, Samson could smell the fear and anxiety on them already, but he didn't tell his mistress this.

Lord Lancer seemed to speak Surah's thoughts. "My daughter makes the second murder in two days," he said. "Something very serious is going on here, and we need answers."

Surah didn't miss the fact that his eyes flicked to her as he said this. There were nods of approval and mumbles of agreement. She cleared her throat.

"We offer our sincere condolences for your losses, my lords and ladies." She looked to her father and put a hand on his shoulder. He reached up and covered her hand with his own. "We have all suffered too much death lately." She looked back to the crowd, swallowing back just enough of her grief to keep the tears out of her eyes and still show her empathy. "And I intend to see the loss stop here."

"This is Black Heart's work," Lady Nightborn called out, swiping at the black smudges under her eyes. Her voice was clear and strong but laced with pain. Surah's respect for the lady grew at this. Most Highborn ladies held their tongues in such meetings.

"We all know he's behind this," Lady Nightborn continued, "and he has gone too far. He must be brought to justice." Her small, gloved fists clenched at her sides.

Now there were outright shouts of approval, and Samson swished his tail around him as he sat by Surah's side. Surah placed her free hand on his back for comfort.

She took another deep breath, her mind flashing back to an hour ago when she had seen Black Heart standing beside Charlie. When Charlie had escaped with him. When things had gone from not good to worse.

Now, her people were calling for blood, and she couldn't blame them. Hadn't she gone off to kill the man who murdered Syris just a month ago against her father's orders?

No, she couldn't blame them, but she still wasn't sure *whom* to blame, and it was her job to find out.

She was also not supposed to mention Charlie's escape. As of right now, three people knew about Black Heart's acquisition of his brother, and she wanted to keep it that way. She opened her mouth, not sure what to say, but knowing it was her turn to speak.

"I will find him," she said, her soft voice carrying sweetly and strongly through the room. "And if he is responsible for this, he will pay."

She could see by the looks on their faces that they were going to hold her to that.

11

SURAH

"Surah, sweetheart, may I have a word with you?" King Syrian asked, after all the people had left the room.

Theo gave a low bow and left, too, leaving her alone with her father and Samson, who spoke up in her head.

"Run for it, love. I've got a feeling this isn't a conversation you want to have."

Surah ignored him, rather than snapping at him about how that was not in the least helpful.

"Of course," she told her father, taking a seat on the arm of his throne, smoothing her cloak out delicately beneath her.

Syrian looked a little peaked, his cheeks slightly red and complexion very pale. She could tell he was thinking about her brother, one of those moments when the grief just seemed to slam into him harder. She was well acquainted with it. She took her glove off her right hand and touched her father's forehead. He was a bit feverish. Her heart seemed to skip a beat.

"It's going to be all right, father," she said, giving him a small smile, which he returned. "I'll figure this out."

He took her hand and kissed it, looking up at his last

remaining child with genuine love. "I know that, Surah. I know." He coughed into his hand, a deep hack that shook in his chest.

Surah's brow creased, heart skipping once more.

"You should lie down," she said. "You don't sound well."

Syrian waved a hand. "There is no time to rest now, dear. Too much to be done. There is a matter I want to discuss with you."

He coughed again, and Surah couldn't say why, but her gut twisted at the sound of it. Syrian's next words shocked her out of whatever she was going to say about it.

"I want you to consider accepting Theodine Gray's proposal for marriage."

Surah stood up involuntarily, the movement less graceful than was her custom, and paced over to Samson, who had a look on his face that said *told you so.* Surah resisted the urge to thump him on the head. Now her heart wasn't skipping, but racing.

For a moment she couldn't think of a single thing to say.

Then, she said, "Surely you don't expect me to consider this while the Black Stone is missing and Highborn women are being murdered." Her tone bordered accusatory, and when her father coughed again she felt bad for this, but it was better than voicing the *Gods no!* that was resounding in her head.

Syrian removed a handkerchief from beneath his cloak and coughed into it. He saw there were spots of red on it when he removed it from his mouth at the same time Surah did. He tried to hide it from her sight, but she stepped forward quickly and snatched the white cloth from his hand. Her heart dropped as she looked down at the smattering of blood there.

Her breath came short, her voice falling to just above a whisper. "What is this, father?" she asked, holding the handkerchief up for him to see. "What is ailing you?"

Syrian eyed the cloth with distaste, and Surah could tell by his face that he had been keeping this from her. He seemed to be unable to find his words. Samson crept forward and sniffed at the blood on the cloth, his amber eyes were tender as they flicked to her.

"I smell demon poison in his blood," Samson told her. *"He must have been scratched or bitten."*

Even in her own head Surah's voice sounded far away as she stared at her tiger. *"Are you sure, Sam?"*

"Quite sure, love."

Surah's heart clenched as she looked at her father. Her voice sounded robotic and far away to her own ears. "Where is it?" she asked.

Syrian released a heavy sigh, as if he would really rather not show her, then pulled the collar of his cloak aside, exposing his shoulder. Four long, ugly scratches were raked across the skin there, an angry red color puckering the edges. The centers of the gashes were black, giving a visual of the poison inside his body.

Surah's hand came up and covered her mouth, her breath catching in her throat. She gave no effort to try and repress her reaction. She didn't even think to.

She stripped the glove from her other hand and gripped his arm, leaning in close to get a better look.

"You've tried healing it?" Her voice still sounded funny, as if she could hear it outside of herself. Stress seemed to keep mounting and mounting in the past two days.

"Of course I've tried healing it," Syrian said, gently removing Surah's hold and replacing the collar of his cloak, hiding the ugly marks.

Surah's heart hurt, actually *hurt,* as she looked at her father, into the violet of his eyes, which were the same color as her own. He was all she had left as far as family went, and her heart knew those scratches were death marks.

Unless she could find the Black Stone. Black magic was the only thing that could heal a demon poisoning, and Surah could see on her father's face that he had already thought of this.

"You tried using the White Stone?" she asked anyway.

Syrian smiled at this silly question. "Yes," he said. "But we both know it was futile."

Surah had figured this, but she still had hoped. Her mouth fell open, wanting to ask him why he hadn't told her, why he hadn't mentioned the urgency of her success in the mission ahead of her.

Instead, she leaned forward and kissed her father's brow, which was warm and clammy under her lips. Syrian gave a small smile and patted her hand. Surah straightened her back, taking a deep breath, trying for her composure.

"I will find it, father," she said, and swallowed. "I promise."

Syrian smiled again. "I know you will, Surah. I know."

The trust in his eyes made her heart hurt more still. He coughed into his hand, using his magic to summon another kerchief, which went to his mouth a clean white and returned splattered with red.

He eyed the mess and crumpled it in his fist, regarding his daughter with gentle eyes. "Think about what I said. Please."

Surah nodded, but instead of thinking about Theo, what she thought was, *I'm coming to find you, Charlie Redmine, and Gods help us both when I do.*

SURAH

There was a knock on her door. Samson raised his head from his paws.

Surah shot him a look telling him to relax, then flicked her wrist and opened the door. Theodine Gray stood there. Her heart picked up in pace at the sight of him, but it wasn't a pleasant feeling.

"And you tell me to relax," Samson said in her head, the smirk clear in his tone.

Surah bit back a response and offered the Head Hunter her best princess-smile. "Are you ready?" she asked.

Theo bowed to her, then nodded. "Yes, my lady. Whenever you are."

Next, Surah called her two personal guards into the room. Noelani entered first, her sharp, pretty face set into Hunter mode, making her look older than usual. She wore a black cloak, the hood covering aqua-colored hair that was cut close on both sides of her head. She bowed to Surah.

Lyonell followed on her heels, his expression as serious as his wife's, his large shoulders just a little too tight, his mouth set into a grim line. Surah had already filled them both in, and they were determined to protect her in her mission, though she thought she could move faster on this if she could work alone. But they were having none of that, not after the thing she had pulled when she went to avenge Syris, and after over two decades of having them as her protectors, she knew arguing would be futile.

Lyonell bowed to his princess as well. "We are ready when you are, my lady," he said.

Surah nodded, wishing again that she could just take Samson and do this by herself. But her father's life was on the line, and she wasn't stupid enough to refuse the help. She took a deep breath and looked up at Bassil, who was standing next to her.

"I need eagle's blood to find the Black Stone," she said, and the Warlock nodded at the others, confirming this. "I am normally opposed to the use of black magic," she continued, "as it stands against the beliefs of our people, but certain circumstances call for certain actions. I do not *want* to find the Black Stone, I *have* to find it," she paused. "And I will do whatever it takes."

Everyone in the room nodded their agreement, as she'd known they would.

She gave another nod, this one somehow more final, as if the show were just really about to begin.

"All right, good," she said. "Step one is acquiring some blood from a Great Eagle, because I will need it to perform a spell to locate the Black Stone." Surah's face was set hard as she looked at them. "You all understand what sort of task this is?"

Nods all around.

"Good. You also understand how *urgent* this task is?"

Immediate agreement.

Surah brought her hands out of her robe and held them out to Noelani and Lyonell, who gripped them with unquestioning trust. Theo stood independently in front of her, gray eyes staring deep into hers.

Bassil touched her shoulder. She turned her head to look at him. Once again, the look on the Warlock's face made a chill crawl down her spine.

"You need at least a pint, princess," Bassil said, his deep rumbling voice as grave as the dead.

Surah nodded, silently steeling herself for what was ahead. Samson unfolded himself from his relaxed position by the window and moved lithely over to where his mistress stood, his head held low, amber eyes surveying the room. He slid in between Surah and Lyonell, forcing the two of them to reach to maintain hold of each other's hands.

The tiger's huge head turned as he looked over at Surah, brushing against her side with his enormous body. *"Let's go, love,"* he said. *"I am born of the Wildlands. Do not fear what waits there. I am the greatest when it comes to Great Beasts. The eagle's blood will be yours."*

Surah could barely hear him over the sound of her heart beating out of her chest, and the silent confession she gave just before zipping them out of the room surprised even her when it sounded in her head.

"But I am scared, Sam. I am."

Samson brushed his head against the hood of her cloak, his warm breath caressing her face, coarse whiskers scratching her skin.

"I know, my love. I know."

IT HAD BEEN SO LONG since she'd been here, but as soon as she felt the warm air against her skin, all the memories of the place came rushing back to her.

The smell was incredibly green, like flowers and thick grass and fresh rain. The jungle trees loomed overhead, casting millions of shadows around every curve, giving the place a late day hue, even though the sun wouldn't set for another six hours.

Tree branches rustled, birds called, and water rushed somewhere in the distance. The Wildlands was a beautiful place, untouched by people and left to flourish under its own rules, but it was also a dangerous place, where the beasts also lived under their own rules.

Noelani and Lyonell already had their swords at the ready, their stances relaxed but alert as they took in the scene around them. Theo's weapon was still concealed beneath his cloak, but Surah could see the tension in his shoulders no matter how much he tried to hide it. She could feel the tension in her own.

Samson moved forward first, his head raised as he tested the air. Surah moved alongside him, gesturing the others behind her, where they would watch her back. They would need to move as a unit if they hoped to pass through the jungle without loss. The place held everything from Great Serpents to Great Primates, and "wild" didn't even begin to explain some of their temperaments. They were called beasts for a reason. Samson was the only one Surah knew of that lived peacefully outside of the jungles, and it would be a mistake to think that even he was tame.

"The nests are too high to get a scent," Samson told her. *"You'll have to perform the spell."*

Surah had known this would probably be the case, though she was loathe to do such a thing. The spell would lead to an eagle for sure, but it would also be pissed off, especially if there were little ones nestled inside.

She hadn't done something like this since she rescued Samson as a cub, and that had been just pure luck. Then again, she had been just a young girl then, and she was well seasoned with the magic this time. She took a deep breath.

Gripping the stone around her neck in her right hand, her left resting on Samson's back, where the powerful muscles in his shoulders were bunched and ready, Surah recited a thread-spell to show them the way.

A golden light as small as a pinprick appeared in front of her. Then it shot out ahead in a string of light that looked very much like the golden thread it was named for, revealing the location of the nearest eagle nest. Surah let go of a breath she hadn't realized she'd been holding and looked around at the others.

"Stay together," she said, and began to follow the thread, which slowly laced up and up through the canopy of green.

A tree branch cracked and rustled to their right, much too loud to be a small creature's movement, and all five of their heads whipped in that direction.

They stopped for a moment, their bodies tense, blood flowing hot and hairs standing up on the backs of their necks. Samson let out a low growl that almost made Surah shiver. She swallowed, listened. When nothing else moved or sounded, she pushed her group onward.

Her voice came out just above a whisper. "Move quickly," she said, and was met with four looks that said, rather plainly, "*no shit.*" Oddly, she had to suppress the urge to laugh at this vulgar thought.

They followed the thread, moving as quickly and quietly as they could manage, the thick growth of the jungle floor a maze of vines and roots. Several times someone tripped, but they were standing so close that someone else always caught them before they fell.

Finally, they reached a point where the thread angled directly up into the treetops. Surah craned her head back, searching for the nest, though she knew it was too high to see from the ground—even if it was probably the size of a large bedroom. Surah swallowed at the image, hoping this was the home of a young eagle that hadn't fully grown into its size.

Removing her sais from beneath her cloak, Surah's heart thundered against her ribs. She looked at her companions, her eyes falling on Samson last and settling there.

"Ready?" she whispered.

She took their silence as answer enough. Her fingers were tight around her weapons. She licked her lips and began another spell. In front of her, the enormous pine, its trunk the width of a wagon, began to shake and sway, its branches making a sound like pouring rain, thousands of needles falling from the tree and showering over them in a curtain of green.

A minute later, they heard it, the outraged cry of a Great Eagle from hundreds of feet above their heads. The sound was a screech and caw that was so loud they had to resist the urge to cover their ears. Surah—though she knew this had to be done—immediately found herself wishing she hadn't done it.

She pushed the thought away. There was her father's health to consider. She had no choice here.

She wondered briefly if she had ever had a choice.

The bird crashed through the trees as if descending from heaven, its wide wings spread out to ease its fall. Its enormous talons were outstretched and snapping branches like twigs as it made its way toward earth to investigate who had disturbed its home.

The eagle was even bigger than Surah had been expecting, its wingspan spreading some forty feet, its razor sharp talons terrifyingly large. Its eyes were huge golden orbs, its beak as menacing as Samson's fangs. Surah had only time to breathe one short breath, see the eagle cock its head in that birdlike manner, hear it issue one more enraged screech into the air, and then the beast attacked.

Surah's group scattered like field mice, breaking apart just in time to avoid being plucked from the ground by the bird's enormous claws. The jungle around them grew quiet—*very* quiet, as the bird took to the air again. Surah knew she had to act fast. She had but seconds before the eagle swooped again. She wrapped her hand around the stone at her throat, closing her eyes and hoping like hell Samson would watch out for her.

"I'm here, love." Samson's voice was hardly more than a growl in her head, the sound of his pumping blood almost audible in it. *I will take the eagle's blood. I will take it take it take it!"*

Surah tried to ignore the eagerness in her tiger's tone and concentrate on the holding spell. It would take a lot of energy to subdue a creature of this size. And she could hear it coming now. Sweeping through the air in another strike. Coming.

Breathe deep. Just breathe deep and concentra—

She was ripped from the thought when something wrapped around her body in a vice grip. Her eyes flew open as her feet left the ground, and a moment of pure panic struck as she realized the eagle had seized her. For a split second, she could think of nothing to do, of no way to save herself as awful panic took control of her mind and made the blood rush in her head.

Then, she gained control of herself, as her years had taught her to do, and managed to snap her fingers, which were pinned to her side, and portal herself back to the ground and out of the bird's death grip.

It was a clumsy transition, and she found herself tucking and rolling as she hit the ground, losing the sai still clutched in her left hand along with the other one that had flown free when the bird snatched her. Her shoulder ached where it struck the ground, but she found her feet swiftly, glad to be back on the earth, even if it was a rough landing.

Her mind was clear and focused now, and she called her weapons back to her with her magic. She caught them out of the air and spun around just in time to avoid being grabbed again by the bird. The eagle let out an enormous cry of rage, but this time, it didn't take off again fast enough. Not fast enough to escape Samson, anyway.

The tiger leapt through the air and tackled the eagle to the ground, the two of them rolling in a heap of feathers, fur, talons, and fangs. The bird tore at his back with its sharp beak, making sounds like that of an oversized, angry rooster, somehow much scarier than one would think.

Samson snapped and ripped and clamped with his powerful jaws, roaring out at the injuries he was sustaining under the eagle's strikes. Surah's heart stopped dead in her chest as she watched chunks of fur and huge feathers and red blood spray through the air. She gripped her stone, her concentration strong now for the worry over her tiger. When Samson hurt, she hurt.

She saw it when the spell worked, they all did, and her companions uttered a collective sigh as the eagle's body went stiff, trapped in the holding spell.

It seemed to take Samson a minute to realize the bird had stopped fighting—or maybe he just wasn't done tasting its blood yet—and for a moment, Surah felt fear for the bird. She was sure Samson was going to kill it.

He wanted to. She could read that as easily from him as if the desire were her own. The muscles in the tiger's chest heaved and contracted as he stared down at the motionless bird, scarlet dripping from his formidable incisors.

For a long moment, the world seemed to pause, as if the earth itself were holding its breath; a moment where everything present was as unmoving as the eagle. Then, Samson's long tongue flicked out and licked the bloodstained fur around his mouth, the sound wet and thick.

His eyes didn't leave the great bird, but his head tilted in Surah's direction, and she knew the moment was over, that the eagle would more than likely live through this.

But she needed to move quickly. The jungle was silent around them, eerily so, even though the battle had surely ruffled some feathers. She found herself swallowing a nervous laugh around this dry joke.

She slid her sais into the back of her cloak and removed a pint-sized vial from a pocket hidden inside the velvet folds.

Surah approached the bird, her boots snapping twigs and crunching pine needles like egg shells, moving slower than she would have liked but unable to help it. She knew her spell was working, but she couldn't deny the caution that was pulsing in her body. She suddenly understood why everyone except her always tensed when Samson entered the room. The Great Beasts were just so damn *big*.

Samson didn't leave his position over the eagle, but his eyes flicked to her as she approached. His tongue snaked out and ran over the red on his face again.

"I told you I would take his blood for you, love. I don't know why you even worry."

Surah raised an eyebrow at the tiger, glad that her back was to the others, because she could feel the worry creeping onto her face, though she fought to keep expressionless.

"Looks like he took some blood from you too, Sam," she replied silently. *"You're hurt."*

Samson's eyes went down to her arms, where deep gashes had been cut by the eagle's talons.

"Looks like I'm not the only one. Finish this up so that we can go home and lick your wounds."

Surah smiled as she placed the vial underneath a deep laceration on the bird's underbelly, pushing her hand into his warm feathers to make the blood flow faster. The bottle would fill quickly, and that was good, but it also made her feel bad. The eagle was seriously hurt.

"You mean lick your *wounds,"* she told Samson.

He gave what could have been a toothy grin. *That too.*

"Princess," Theo said, making Surah jump a little before she could stop herself, spilling some of the blood in the nearly full vial and stopping a curse just short in her throat. The others had been so quiet she had nearly forgotten they were even there.

Surah raised her eyebrows at Theo, asking why he was interrupting her, but he was glancing around cautiously, his sword still held at the ready.

"It's time to go," he said, his voice just above a whisper.

Surah heard what was causing the urgency in Theo's tone just as he spoke, and her head whipped to the south. What she saw there made her heart stop dead in her chest, her eyes going wide as the scene took on a sharp focus.

A group of five Great Primates were smashing through the trees, barreling toward them like monster trucks. Their huge fists pounded the earth and shook the ground under their feet, grunts and roars issuing from their enormous mouths.

Surah capped off the vial with quick hands and shoved it back into the pocket inside her cloak, unaware that her jaw was unhinged.

"Yes," she said, her voice incredibly small beneath the sound of the beasts thundering toward them. "I'd say so."

Noelani and Lyonell were at Surah's sides, gripping her hands, and Samson moved next to her in the same heartbeat. Theo was tense and ready to leave as soon as she made the move, but Surah spared one more look for the eagle, whose huge golden eyes seemed to be accusing her from their halted position, where its head lay cocked toward her. Her heart hurt a little seeing the bird so badly injured, knowing she did not have time to heal it, knowing she was leaving it in a terrible position with the primates approaching.

But the decision was clear. The eagle would have to handle its own. Her father was counting on her. Hell, a whole *kingdom* was counting on her.

She broke the holding spell, releasing the bird, and snapped her fingers, transporting her companions out of the Wildlands just seconds before the group of beasts reached them, wishing she could have waited long enough to make sure the eagle got away, hoping it would, and thinking it was probably the least of her worries.

It still hurt, made her feel not very good about herself, but it was the least of her worries, indeed.

13

SURAH

The tiger's rough tongue ran over the cuts on Surah's arms, making her clench her teeth to bite back a wince.

Samson had been literally licking her wounds since she was a child, and though she knew other people would be nervous about having a tiger do this, she wasn't. She knew Samson would never hurt her, not even if he did like the taste of her blood, which he must.

She pulled her arm back and stood from her bed. Samson gave her an annoyed look.

"Okay," she said, "I've had my bath. Now let me heal you. I have business that needs attending."

Samson sat back on his haunches and slid to the floor, licking his paws. *I'm perfectly fine. The bird didn't hurt me.*

Surah coughed into her hand. "Bullshit."

He raised his head. *You really shouldn't mumble and curse, dear. It doesn't become you.*

Surah rolled her eyes. "You sound like the etiquette teachers of my childhood. Now, stop your nonsense and hold still."

She wrapped her hand around the Stone at her throat and

ran her free hand over Samson's wounds, saying the healing spell over and over until the torn skin repaired itself, weaving together slowly like stitch work. The tiger narrowed his eyes to slits and let out low growls as the pain slowly left him.

When it was done, he rubbed his big soft head against Surah's side, knocking her over a bit with his weight.

"Thank you," he said.

Surah ran her fingers through his fur, performing a spell to clean away some of the blood clumped there. Samson gently caught her hand in between his massive jaws, the tips of his long teeth just barely pressing into her skin. She raised an eyebrow at him, and he opened his mouth to release her.

"You have work to do. That's more than enough fussing over me."

Surah said nothing, thinking of the bird she had left so wounded in the jungle, wondering if it had been able to fly away before the gorillas reached it. Samson nudged her with his nose, as if to knock the thoughts away.

"No time for that," he said softly.

"Do you think it got away?" she asked, cringing at the hope in her voice, as if Samson held the definite answer to this.

He licked at some leftover blood on his blue and black paw. *"It put up a hell of a fight."*

Surah released a breath, nodded. "I suppose it did," she said, and then she spoke to him silently, her next words too revealing to be spoken aloud.

"I don't know what to do, Sam. I'm scared. I'm not even sure if I should be, but I am. I can't seem to organize my mind. I don't even know what I'm supposed to be doing. Things are moving too fast."

Samson rose to his paws, his amber eyes watching Surah closely. He leaned in and ran his warm, sandpaper tongue slowly up her cheek. Surah wrapped her arms around his neck and held him tight, burying her face in his thick fur. She was beyond grateful to the universe for allowing her to keep such a great friend. At least it had left her that.

"You know what to do, love. Just one step at a time. Step one, find the Black Stone. Step two, use it to save your father. Three, see that whoever is responsible for the murders meets justice. Easy as one-two-three."

Surah pulled back from him and gave a dry little laugh. She ran a hand though her hair and smoothed out her cloak. "That easy, huh?" she said. "What would I do without your wise guidance?"

Samson's lips pulled up in what Surah knew to be his version of a grin.

"Oh, I don't know. Maybe get fed to baby eagles at the top of a tree in the jungle. That sounds about right."

Surah laughed in earnest now. "I love you, Sam," she said.

"And I you, my love. Now, summon the Warlock and let's take that first step."

Surah nodded, but had a strong feeling that the first steps had already been taken, and that bridges were burning behind them.

1 4

SURAH

*I*t took Surah and Bassil three hours to prepare everything. By that time the sun was finally setting on what had been an incredibly long day.

Surah stared out the window in her chambers, beneath which Samson had reclaimed his position.

The lights of Zadira were just beginning to flicker on out there, the people of her father's kingdom leaving work and heading home for dinner with their families. Down on Side Street, the bands would be striking up and beer would be flowing in the taverns. On the east side of town, mothers would be walking their children home from school. Fathers would be kicking off work boots. At times like this, Surah couldn't help but envy these common people, though she understood well that the grass was always greener.

Bassil eyed her from across the small table where the ingredients to the tracking spell were spread out. He tilted his head as he looked at her. Surah's face was as emotionless as ever.

"Ready, princess?" he asked.

Surah snapped out of her thoughts and rolled her shoulders, nodding. She pulled the hood of her cloak over her head. Even if her face gave nothing away, her heart was thumping. Black magic was something she didn't have much familiarity with. Her teachers over the years, which included her brother, had all been unmovable in their positions regarding the dark arts. This was the common feeling among most of the people—something that was regarded as taboo, not to mention illegal.

She reached out and began pouring the various liquids on the small round table into a bowl at the center, forcing the thoughts of her brother away gently. Wondering what Syris would think of her actions were he still alive would do her no good right now. *Something* needed to be done, and she was doing it. There would be plenty of time for contemplations later, like when her father wasn't slowly dying of demon poisoning and a murderer wasn't on the loose.

The mixture in the bowl let off a pungent scent, filling the room with the smells of burning things and spoiled sugar, almost to a choking capacity. Surah breathed shortly through her mouth and held her hands out to Bassil over the table after adding the last ingredient, the stolen eagle's blood.

The Warlock placed his hand in hers and began the spell, chanting low in the tongue of the ancients, his deep voice a rumble in his chest. Surah looked down at the paper beside her and read along with the words, echoing Bassil in her sweet, soft voice, creating a juxtaposition that sounded eerie to her own ears.

Samson watched from beneath the window, his ears perked and muscles tense.

Their chanting seemed to carry on into oblivion, and after a while, Surah was at the point where she felt like giving up.

Nothing but that terrible smell had been produced by the spell thus far, and she was beginning to think she just couldn't do it. But she carried on a little longer. If this failed, it was back to the drawing board, and she didn't have time for that. Her father didn't have time for that.

In a matter of forty-eight hours the demon poison could be fatal. And that was a highball.

She shoved the doubt away, as she had been doing with a whole range of emotions lately, trying her hardest to concentrate on the spell and the words, trying hard to settle the roiling in her soul. Salty sweat rolled down her back, the weight of the cloak heavy there. She ran her tongue out over her lips, feeling sudden tears of frustration threaten. She swallowed them away.

At last, when she was just thinking she couldn't do this any longer, it happened. Bassil felt it at the same time she did, his large hands tightening around hers to an almost crushing proportion. Surah's heart went from sinking to galloping like a racehorse out of the gate. She stared into the smoke drifting up from the clay bowl, unaware that she was biting down on her lip hard enough to draw blood. The room was silent now, both of them having stopped the chanting on the same syllable.

An image began to form in the smoke, the scene moving like an eagle's eye over the land. Surah swallowed back more tears as the thought reminded her of the bird she had all but left to die.

She stared into the smoke and got the feeling of vertigo as the lens passed over the city, where people were walking the streets and store windows were going dark and the lights of the taverns were blinking to life. It soared over the buildings, over the alleys and backyards of private homes. Then out further still, over the grassland and forests and small towns, and further still and still.

The Black Stone was in the jungles of the Southlands then, because nothing else was out this far. Surah's throat went tight as the smoke scene proved her right, and now she felt the perspiration roll down the side of her face as well. The jungles of the Southlands were even more dangerous than the ones to the north where she had obtained the eagle blood. The things that lived there were more monsters than beasts.

The scene halted over its destination, still high above the

green canopy, where only the shadows penetrated. She could only imagine what could be waiting, hiding there. Then, the picture vanished and was replaced by numbers, which Surah knew were longitude and latitude.

She committed them to memory instantly, letting out a long breath and finally releasing Bassil's hands. He looked as peaked as she probably did, his dark skin having taken on an ashy tone. Surah could tell by the expression on his face that his stomach was as queasy as hers. Black magic had a way of doing that to the user.

But she had what she needed. She knew where she had to go. And time was ticking.

She stood from her chair and ignored the lightheadedness rushing over her in a wave, blinking back a few spots that appeared before her eyes. She ran her hands down her cloak, composing herself, clenching her teeth against the complaining of her stomach.

"Where are you going?" Bassil asked, wiping some sweat from his brow with the back of his hand and settling back in his chair.

Surah raised an eyebrow at the stupid question.

Bassil chuckled and shook his head. "You are not going into the Southland jungle at eleven o'clock at night, especially not if you're feeling as nauseated as I am."

Surah tilted her head, her lips quirked in a small half-smile. She leaned forward, gripping the chair in front of her more for support than effect. Not that she would admit it.

"You're giving me orders now, Warlock?"

Bassil gave her a droll look. "Of course not, dear Princess," he said. "Wouldn't dream of it." He spread his hands. "Go on and get yourself killed if you like. I'll do my best to help your father in your stead."

Surah spoke through her teeth, not really angry with Bassil so much as frustrated and tired and nauseated. "You know I don't have much time. The Black Stone could be moved and then we would be back at square one. This is imminent."

Bassil nodded. "And so is being able to get out of the jungle alive. You really want to walk into that place in the middle of night? Like I said, be my guest. Ignore my council. Gods know you've never had trouble doing that."

Surah knew he was right, that she would need to prepare for this mission, and yes, she needed to rest and eat, since she couldn't remember the last time she'd done so, but that didn't stop a little impatient anger from spiraling in her belly.

"Well," she said, taking a seat on her bed. Samson jumped down from the windowsill and hopped on the bed beside her, making her dip to the side. "You don't have to be such a dick about it."

This made them both laugh, relieving some of the tension that seemed to have been brewing in the air for the last couple days. Bassil stood and bowed to her before taking his leave.

"Sleep, princess," he said, "I will let the Head Hunter know you want to leave at first light." He checked the magical sundial that hung from a chain inside his cloak. "That'll give you a little over six hours to rest. I think you should sleep longer, but I know you won't."

Surah looked at him, letting her mask slip for just a moment because she couldn't help it. "I don't think I can sleep at all, Bassil," she said, and hated that her voice sounded small.

The Warlock gave her a gentle smile and opened the door to leave. "Try, princess. Just try," he said. "That's all anyone can ask of you." Then the door clicked shut behind him.

After he left, Surah kicked off her boots and slung her cloak over the chair by the window, crawling into her big bed beside Samson, who took up most of it, and snuggled into his warm fur. She felt very alone right then, as she had for a good portion of her life, very alone and very tired, but she was right about not being able to sleep despite her exhaustion. How could she?

Things seemed to be getting worse and worse with every passing moment, drifting further up the creek and losing paddles.

She clenched her jaw and closed her eyes, trying not to think about all the people she had lost over the years, her brother, her sister, her mother. Trying not to think about the possibility of losing her father as well.

Trying—and this was somehow the most disturbing of all—not to think about Charlie Redmine. The man with the penetrating emerald gaze and the criminal brother who seemed hellbent on causing trouble.

No, she should not be thinking about those things at all.

15

SURAH

When she awoke, Charlie Redmine was standing in her room.

"Would you like me to kill him for you, love? I will gladly kill him for you."

For a few moments, Surah couldn't seem to form another thought, she just sat on the bed staring wide-eyed at the scene in front of her, her mouth hanging open as she sucked in air. There was no thought for composure.

Samson was staring at Charlie, but Charlie was staring at her, his hands raised in surrender, his back pushed up against the wall, only his wide chest moving with his deep breaths.

She'd been dreaming about the day they'd first met, and it was somehow paralyzing to wake from that dream, where the emerald color of his eyes had been so crystal, and come back into reality and see them with even more clarity there. To go from looking at him as the boy she'd helped escape to the man—very, *very* much a man—standing within her bedroom.

About to be eaten by her tiger.

She opened her mouth to say something, but instead, spoke

to Samson in her head, practically tripping over the words to get them across. *"No, don't kill him."*

The tiger's only response was a small grumble, but he held his position between Charlie and his mistress.

Surah climbed out of bed and grabbed her cloak from the chair beside it, wrapping it around her shoulders and feeling a little better with the weight of her sais on her back. She used her magic to return her boots to her feet. Then she just stood there like an idiot. Now what?

When Charlie spoke, his voice was deep and low, cautious. "I come in peace, princess."

Surah still didn't know what to say, so when she opened her mouth, even she was surprised by what came out. "Are you insane, Charlie?"

Whoops. She hadn't meant to call him that.

One side of his mouth quirked at this, but his hands were still raised, and Samson was practically breathing in his face. "It's nice to see you again too, Surah."

This snapped her out of whatever trance she'd been in. She stalked forward, removing one of the sais from her back and clutching it in her right hand.

"Do not speak to me like that," she said, all her anger over the events of the past two days rushing back to her. "I am your princess. You will address me as such."

Charlie said nothing to this, just stared at her in that annoyingly mysterious way he had, and Surah ignored the fact that she felt a little guilty at the harshness of her tone. Why should she feel guilty? Highborn ladies were being murdered, her father was dying, and she knew his brother and him had something to do with it. She just *knew* it.

"Where is the Black Stone?" she asked, fully expecting him to evade the question.

He didn't. "My brother has it."

Surah's brow furrowed as she was taken aback, not sure

what to think of this blatantly honest answer. She found herself fumbling again for her words. "Why are you here?"

His next answer sounded as honest as the first, but Surah wasn't naive enough to let that make her think it couldn't be a lie. She happened to be a master at deceit as well.

"I've come to help you stop him," Charlie said.

"Why?" Her voice came out smaller than she would have liked, even though both of their tones had yet to reach above a whisper.

"I don't know," he said.

Surah raised her eyebrows, still holding the sai in her right hand. "That's reassuring."

"Your father's sick, right?" he asked, and Surah's eyes narrowed. He continued on before she could say anything. "You want my help or not?"

Her teeth clenched, and she raised her weapon for the first time and pointed it at him, her violet eyes as hard as stones. No one spoke to her so plainly. Except maybe her father.

"What makes you think I need your cooperation? I could kill you right now. You obviously have a hand in all this."

Charlie shrugged, as if it didn't matter either way. "You could, and actually, I don't."

They were silent for a moment, and Samson spoke in her head. *"Are you going to invite him to tea, my love, or do you want me to tear his throat out?"*

"I don't know yet."

"You're oddly indecisive with this one."

"I know."

A pause.

"Be careful."

"I'm trying."

Charlie spoke in that easy way of his. "I'm sorry about everything that's happening, princess, but I'm here to help you. If you want to have me locked up," his eyes flicked to Samson, "or kill me, that's your choice."

Surah found herself looking at his lips and instead met his gaze. "You just want me to trust you?"

His eyes seemed to pin her, even though he was the one who was pinned, his voice as calm as if they were just sharing tea. "That's what you wanted me to do, and I did."

"You think I'm a fool."

He shook his head once, slowly. "Not at all." In a mumble, he added, "*I'm* the one being a damn fool."

Surah looked out her window, trying to make a decision—any decision—and saw with a drop of her heart that the sun was making an appearance over the horizon, the first light of the new day. Bassil or Theo would be here soon, expecting her to be ready to set off to the jungles of the Southlands, where the eagle's blood had traced the Black Stone.

She approached Charlie now, feeling the urgency in her movements. If she didn't make a decision here soon, the decision would be made for her.

She stepped up beside Samson and held her hand out to Charlie, her face grave and beautiful. He gave her his hand, his inscrutable gaze locked on hers.

"Are you planning to betray me?" she asked, hoping he would pass her lie detector test and also hoping he wouldn't. Somehow she knew that his answer would seal an envelope, though she still had no idea what was tucked inside it.

"No," he said.

Just then, there was a knock at her door, and all three of their heads whipped in that direction.

"Time's up," Samson told her. *"What do you want to do?"*

Charlie watched her closely, said nothing,

In the end, it was Samson who made the decision.

"Let's see what he has to say. You obviously want to. If he tries to

betray you, I'll kill him. But you better take us out of here now, love. Whoever is calling won't wait much longer."

Before she could question her tiger's council or her own warring thoughts, Surah gripped Charlie's hand, which still held hers, and placed her other one on Samson's shoulder.

The door swung open and Theodine Gray entered just a split second after Surah squeezed her eyes shut and portaled the three of them out of the room, feeling like she was falling over a ledge into a gorge that would be impossible to climb out of rather than flying through space and time.

It felt very much like falling, indeed.

16

SURAH

They landed in a large forest just outside Zadira, where only the woodland creatures and the occasional hunter roamed.

The sun was slowly making its ascent in the sky, filtering through the trees in streams of golden light. The forest was quiet this morning, with only the sound of squirrels jumping from branches and birds calling from their nests.

Charlie stumbled a little when Surah released his hand, bending over and clutching his knees at the feeling of vertigo that came with the sudden departure. Samson stood very close to her side, watching Charlie with a slightly amused expression behind his eyes.

Charlie straightened up, boldly giving Samson a look that said he knew the tiger was enjoying this. Surah couldn't help but be a little impressed at his bravery. People didn't just look at Samson any way they wanted. Only she did that. It made her wonder just who Charlie Redmine really was. She couldn't get a read on the man.

She crossed her arms over her chest. "Start talking," she said.

Charlie stared at her for a moment, and she didn't like the

fact that she had to plant her feet to keep from shifting under his gaze.

"My brother has the Black Stone, and he wants you and your father dead."

For a moment, she was at a loss for words again. She wondered if his blunt way of delivering information had that effect on everyone. She was usually quicker on her feet.

"Wonderful," she said, "and you escaped his clutches to come tell me this? How did you get into my room?"

Charlie reached up and pulled out a necklace that had been tucked under his shirt. On the end of the chain was a small piece of the Black Stone, not enough to cure her father, but enough to portal somewhere, like right outside her bedroom window, even with all the spells around the castle blocking the travel.

Her eyes narrowed. "How'd you get that?"

"Michael gave it to me."

"Michael?"

"My brother…Black Heart, I guess."

"Why would he do that?"

"Because I told him I would help him."

She raised an eyebrow at this. "And instead you've come to help me."

"That's about the short of it."

"Well, forgive me, Mr. Redmine, but the 'short of it' sounds like bullshit."

"It's not."

Surah threw her hands up, looking at Samson for an answer.

The tiger gave her a look that conveyed his amusement. "*Do you want me to decide everything, love? I can, but at some point I might decide to just eat him, and something tells me you wouldn't like that.*"

"*Who says I would care?*" she snapped silently.

Samson gave his version of a grin. "*You don't have to.*"

Charlie was watching them as if he could hear their silent conversation. As if he was the only one with mysteries.

"Are we going to stand here all day?" Charlie asked. "Or do you want to get going on saving your father?"

Surah sighed, trying not to look at Charlie too closely, seriously afraid that she was making a huge mistake here. She shouldn't be doing this, and she knew it. But no one had talked to her this way since Syris died, and Charlie's blunt, certain way of speaking had a way of making her listen. It had absolutely nothing to do with his wide shoulders and muscled arms and mysterious emerald eyes and perpetually calm manner. Nothing at all.

"I suppose you have a plan on how to do that?" she asked.

"To help you save your father? Yeah, you could say that."

"And then what?"

Charlie was silent for a moment, his handsome face carefully expressionless. "I can't help you catch and kill my brother, if that's what you're asking," he said. "I'll help you save your father, but I can't do that."

Surah swallowed and licked her lips. "Alright," she said, "Help me save my father, and I won't ask you to."

She wasn't sure if this was a lie or not, but it sounded true, so that was good. She had come this far, and the clock was still ticking. Step one was curing her father. She could decide on step two when the time came.

Charlie nodded. "Okay." He took a step toward her, a slow one, his eyes flicking to Samson, and held out his hand to Surah. "Let's go, then."

Surah just looked at him for a moment, studying the dark, trimmed facial hair that covered his strong jaw and surrounded his soft-looking mouth. The unwarranted thought that came next scared her more than anything else that had happened in the last two days.

The thought was, she wondered what that course hair would feel like against her skin, how his lips would feel against it, too.

The realization that he wasn't just a handsome man, but a rather *gorgeous* one was even worse. Her eyes wandered down Charlie's body before she could help it, and that was probably the very first time that she knew she was in serious trouble here.

Samson's head tilted toward her, and she cursed silently as she realized the tiger knew what she was thinking. She must have been projecting the thoughts pretty clear. She had to watch it.

"Where are we going?" she asked, using great effort to sound as sure and strong as she didn't at all feel.

Charlie reached down and took her hand, the movement as sure and unhesitant as his words. Samson shocked the magic out of her for letting Charlie do this. People didn't just reach out and touch their princess without permission.

She shocked herself even more when *she* didn't protest.

"Shopping," he said, and when he smiled, perfect white teeth peeking out behind those lips, Surah's heart flipped. There was nothing she could do to stop it. "Do you like to go shopping, princess?"

Surah knew he was trying to lighten the mood, but her mood was anything but light at the moment. The expression on her face was as blank as a fresh sheet of parchment. She said nothing. But she didn't pull her hand away from him, either. And when the thought came to her that she wished she weren't wearing her gloves, so that she could feel his touch again, she chastised herself in her own mind like an angry mother.

Her silence seemed to have no effect on him. "We have to be careful, though," he continued.

Surah gave him a droll look, ignoring the hammering of her heart.

His small smile returned. "We'll need some things if we hope to pass through the Southlands and get what we need for your father. This means we have to go somewhere you'll be recognized in a second."

Surah nodded and snapped the fingers of her free hand. Charlie watched with wide eyes as her hair went from long lavender to a short, pale blond, the violet leaking out of her eyes and leaving them a dull brown color. Her facial features shifted slightly, making her look ten years older and not like herself at all. Even her attire changed; her rich cloak faded into an old, used black. She couldn't help a small smile at the amazement on his face.

Samson seemed to be grinning, too.

"Well, I'll be damned," Charlie said.

Surah said nothing, but as she stared into those deep eyes of his, a strange feeling of fluttering and tightening in her gut, her breath catching in her throat, what she thought was, *we both may be.*

17

THEO

Theo knocked once more on the princess's chamber door, the sound of his knuckles rapping on the wood echoing down the windowless hallway, thinking that she was probably just rousing from her sleep.

When still he heard no movement or response from beyond the door, his lips pinched together as he let out a sigh and looked at Lyonell, who stood guard to the right, Noelani to the left.

Lyonell shrugged. "Probably sleeping," he said.

Theo gave him an impatient look and reached for the door, but Noelani stepped in front of him, ignoring the plain anger that passed behind the Head Hunter's eyes. She met his glare evenly.

"I'll check on the princess," she said. "She may not be decent."

Theo was unhappy about being interrupted, his face smooth but hard-lined, and he waved a hand to tell her to get on with it, then. Noelani opened the door to Surah's room and pushed her way inside.

She returned a moment later.

"She's gone," Noelani said, and had to jump out of the way so as not to be knocked over when Theo charged into the room.

The Head Hunter's eyes went to the empty, ruffled bed, the window, the bathroom. As they flicked from place to place a darkness seemed to pass over his expression, his lips pulling down and his eyes narrowing in his masculine face. For a moment, he said nothing, but both Noelani and Lyonell could see this was in great effort of controlling himself.

When he spoke, it was between clenched teeth. "Where did she go?" he asked.

At that moment, Bassil entered the room, moving in that eerily silent way the big Warlock seemed to have perfected, his patchwork cloak rippling with his movements. His deep voice sounded almost amused when he spoke. Almost, but not quite.

"Wherever she pleased, I would assume," Bassil said.

Theo's head whipped toward him, the Head Hunter's distaste toward the Warlock evident on his face.

Theo's voice was almost a growl now. "She should not be alone right now. Highborn women are being murdered."

The Warlock lifted his wide shoulders once and dropped them. "The princess can take care of herself," he said.

Noelani spoke up, ignoring Lyonell's look that asked her to stay silent. "The princess is not a prisoner here. She can leave whenever she likes."

When Theo looked at her, Noelani did not shrink under the cold gray of his eyes. She only held his stare and raised her chin a fraction. Theo had to give it to the female Hunter; men much bigger than her had withered under his gaze.

Instead of barking at her, Theo regarded Bassil again, which he could see enraged Noelani almost as much as if he'd hit her. He wouldn't hit a woman, but he was very good at dismissing them.

"Have you performed the tracking spell?" Theo asked.

The Warlock shook his head. "We didn't have a chance yet," he said.

For some reason, Theo got the feeling that he was lying, but Bassil's position was a high one in the court, and accusing him of lying would be seen as a major insult.

Theo was silent a moment, trying to think of his next move. Ordinarily, as Head Hunter he was to await orders from the Keeper before making any decisions or pursuits, but this was not an *ordinary* situation. Syris—who'd been the best Keeper Theo had ever known—was no longer here. And while he may be in love with Surah, he was not the type of man who completely trusted a woman to these kinds of matters.

These kinds of matters were between life and death. High-born ladies were being murdered. King Syrian was poisoned with demon blood. The Black Stone was missing. No, this was no job for a woman. Women had soft hearts. Theo didn't think this was a bad thing, an insult to females, rather just the way it was and was supposed to be. A natural balance. He would need to lead this case. Besides, the princess could end up getting hurt.

Then there was Charlie Redmine. Fucking Charlie Redmine. How long had it been since he'd seen that country, common scum? A long time, he supposed. But not long enough. He knew that son of a bitch had something to do with this, had known it right off the bat, even before he and the princess had witnessed Redmine escape with Black Heart. Yes, he would need to put a stop to all of this, punish those who were responsible.

Not only that, but he hated the way that common shithead had looked at Surah. He *hated* it.

But there was protocol to follow, or at least appear to follow as long as he could stand to. He would wait for the princess to show back up for a few hours, and then he would take the coordinates that Bassil knew and go searching for the Stone.

"She could just be in with King Syrian," Lyonell said, cutting into the Head Hunter's thoughts.

Theo's teeth clenched, but his tone was composed, his face smooth, even amicable. It was a wonder how much control one could gain from a highly disciplined lifetime, but there was nothing he could do to stop the dark emotions from storming through his head.

"I just left King Syrian," he said.

Noelani chimed in. "I'm sure she'll return shortly."

Now Theo very much wanted to tell her to shut up, but being a woman, she would probably run back to the princess and tattle-tell on him. And that surely wasn't the best way to convince her to be his wife.

He nodded, giving an indulgent smile. "Of course," he said. "We'll wait for her then."

Then he swept out of the room, his heavy cloak swaying behind his swift, sure steps, leaving the two Hunters and the Warlock standing in the princess's chambers and staring silently at each other. Beyond the arched windows, the early morning light strengthened with the rise of a new day.

Theo walked down the hallway that led back to the foyer, listening to the click of his boot heels on the polished hardwood floor and the blood that was pulsing in his ears.

He would wait for the princess, all right. He would wait for exactly three hours.

And then he would go looking for her.

18

SURAH

*S*urah stood staring at the small stone cottage, her heart thumping nervously in her chest. The silence of the place is what struck her first, surrounding her so completely in an instant.

Green vines sporting yellow flowers crawled up the front of the little house, framing the door and two square windows. The path leading up to the porch was collaged stone, red and gray and black that fit together in a sort of mosaic. The only sound was the wind rustling through the long grasses all around them.

The sunlight was beginning to strengthen, reminding Surah that the clock on her father's life was still ticking. She took one more moment to take in her surroundings, looking all around in every direction and seeing no other civilization in sight, just miles and miles of green and yellow grasslands.

"Where did you bring me?" she asked, avoiding Charlie's eyes, wishing she didn't feel like she had to. She gestured to the cottage with one gloved hand, the glamour she was wearing making her expensive glove look old and tattered. "This doesn't look like any shop I've ever seen."

Charlie began striding up the stone path to the cottage in

that sure way of his, and Surah found that she had no problem looking at him when he wasn't looking back. She decided against her will that she liked the way the denim of his jeans sat below his waist, how she had never known that such common attire could be attractive. She personally had never donned a pair of jeans in her life, and she wondered if her rear end would look as good in them.

When she looked over and saw Samson staring at her, she shut those thoughts off like a faucet.

"Eyes on the prize," the tiger told her silently. *"Don't trust this man, princess."*

"I know what I'm doing and I don't trust him."

"Good."

Charlie climbed the steps of the cottage and turned to look at her. "You coming?" he asked.

Surah remained where she was, her hand resting on the tiger's shoulder. "Not until you tell me what I'm walking into. You still haven't told me anything about this plan of yours, Mr. Redmine. I'd like to hear it."

Charlie moved back down the steps and stopped in front of her. Surah had to swallow twice to hold his gaze. His deep, low voice seemed to fill up the world in the emptiness around them, those emerald-colored eyes burning. Always burning.

"This is a friend's house, my lady," he said. "I've known Carolyn for over five years. She deals in the kinds of items we'll be needing."

Surah just looked at him, her face carefully expressionless. "What kinds of items would that be?"

Charlie was silent for a moment. "I think you know."

"The use of black magic is forbidden in my father's kingdom, Mr. Redmine. I would have assumed you knew this."

Charlie nodded once, either completely ignoring her incredulity or not hearing it. She couldn't tell. She just couldn't get a read on this man.

"Sure," he said, "but I would assume that you know Michael is using black magic to stay hidden and to keep...unwanted people away. How do you propose we get anywhere near the Stone without using it, too? I suppose I just assumed that you wouldn't be opposed to it with your father's life on the line."

Surah's teeth clenched. Charlie Redmine clearly had no manners or concern for social status, and she found the thought flying out of her mouth before she could stop it.

"You've got some nerve, Mr. Redmine, speaking to me the way you do."

Charlie said nothing to this, just sighed and rubbed a hand down his slightly scruffy jaw. He looked as exasperated as she felt. Meanwhile, Samson looked slightly bored and amused at the whole thing.

Charlie looked at her now, his eyebrows raised. "Make up your mind, princess," he said. "Are you going to trust me or not?"

Surah tilted her chin up a fraction. "Not," she said, and began striding up to the cottage with her perfect posture and sure steps. Samson followed at her side. She was just about to knock on the door when Charlie spoke from behind her.

"He should stay out here," he said, and Surah glanced over her shoulder to see he was talking about Samson. "If Carolyn sees him, she'll know who you are, even with all that glamour. No one else in the kingdom owns a beast like that."

"I do not *own* Samson," she said.

Charlie Redmine seemed to have a knack for pissing her off, even with all her hard gained composure.

Samson surprised her by chuckling in her head, the sound a deep, growling rumble. *"Sure you do, love. Sure you do."*

"He shouldn't be speaking to me this way," she told him silently, her tone more of a snap than she intended.

Surah thought if Samson could have shrugged, he would have. He hopped off the porch and began walking to the back of the house, his head held low as he sniffed at the green and yellow grasses.

"Isn't that what you're always complaining about?" He asked her as he slipped into the field to the east of the cottage, the amusement clear in his tone. *"I thought you wanted to be treated like everyone else. Sometimes you just have to give an inch, princess. I'm not saying trust him, just give an inch."*

Surah sighed and looked at Charlie, who was silent, which seemed to be his way. Looking at her as if he were the one having some secret, internal conversation. She wished he wouldn't look at her. She could feel his gaze on her skin, something that stroked rather than just saw, and her returning thought to Samson surprised even her. She regretted it as soon as it was born.

"I know that's what I wanted, and that's why I wish he wouldn't do it."

The tiger stopped in his tracks, the long grasses brushing against his powerful legs, the strengthening daylight casting a heavenly light around his blue and black striped body. His head turned, ears swiveling gracefully, and Surah thought the look Samson gave her when his amber eyes met hers was sort of painful. Then he turned and slunk into the grasses, body held low. A bit of real fear spiraled in her gut. She refused to examine the question *fear of what?*

Surah turned back to Charlie, her chin slightly raised. When he just stood there unmoving, she waved her hand impatiently to tell him to get on with it. Just because she didn't trust him didn't mean she didn't intend to see where he led her. As of right now, he seemed to be the most direct path to the Stone she needed to save her father, and she was fully prepared to kill him if worse came to worst.

At least, she thought she was.

Charlie climbed the porch steps once more, flashing Surah that charming smile of his when she moved away before his shoulder could brush hers. He reached up and knocked on the wooden door, which thumped hollowly. Surah had to stop herself from shifting her feet as they waited, despite the fact that she was not a shifty person.

A minute passed, then two, and another. Surah was a split second away from telling Charlie to knock again when the door swung open, the hinges creaking in a way that would have been comical if not for the uneasy feeling in her stomach. It was an oddly gripping sound.

The smell that wafted out of the cottage and bombarded Surah's senses was that of rich flowers and thick herbs, stale smoke and spoiled milk. It rolled out toward her on a wave that made her eyes water and her throat itch, and no amount of etiquette training could keep her nose from wrinkling. She covered her mouth on the shoulder of her cloak just in time to catch the three sneezes that forced their way out.

She almost summoned a handkerchief before she thought better of it. She was in disguise, and common people didn't use the magic in such frivolous ways, and if she did summon one she wasn't sure she would be able to keep from covering her mouth and nose with it anyway. And that sort of delicate, royal behavior was not going to cut it here.

She loosened her shoulders, adding a slight slump to her back, breaking her perfect posture. Maintaining the magic that held her false appearance in place was not the hard part— though it wasn't *easy* by anyone's standards. The hard part would be not conducting herself like a princess.

A voice issued from the darkness inside the cottage, where the only light was from the two dusty square windows that shed dirty streams of sunlight into the room. The voice was soft and low, a woman's, that of deep trolling bells. The sound of it made an unexplained chill crawl up Surah's spine, but she didn't allow herself to shiver.

"Charlie?" the voice said. "That you, Charlie Redmine?"

The room filled with light then, the four torches on the walls coming to life and illuminating the contents of the place.

Surah's eyes flicked around the room, settling on the stacks of old books, the jars and vials set on the shelves that held various substances, the old leather couch and armchair, and finally on the carved table in the corner, where the owner of that deep bell voice sat.

Surah's first thought upon seeing Carolyn was that she was an extreme juxtaposition to her home. Her hair was a long, yellow blond, hanging in soft waves over shoulders that sported a rich black cloak. Her face was fine lines and delicate curves, with plush pink lips and big crystal blue eyes. Her makeup was applied perfectly, her hands ungloved but clean with blood-red fingernails. The woman stood in one smooth movement, her back held straight and her cloak flowing around her gracefully. A smile lit up her face as her eyes settled on Charlie.

She held her arms out to him the way a mother might do a long lost child. *Or the way a lover might a long lost flame,* Surah thought, then shoved the whole matter out of her mind. Focus was key here. Eyes on the prize.

"Charlie Redmine," the woman said, coming forward, arms still outstretched. "I'll be damned by the Gods. It is you."

Surah resisted raising an eyebrow. This woman was a whole bucket of juxtaposition, it seemed. Her foul, common way of speaking matched her house but not her appearance.

Charlie stepped into the cottage, his face giving away no indication that he could even smell the foul mixture of scents that invaded the room. He went over to Carolyn and pulled her into a hug that Surah thought lasted too long, knowing she had no business feeling that way at all, averting her eyes from the two of them and standing outside the open door in awkward silence.

"It's good to see you, too, Carolyn," Charlie said, stepping back from her and offering her that charming smile. "You look good."

The way Carolyn smiled and fluttered her eyelashes in return answered one of Surah's earlier questions. So Charlie Redmine did have an effect on other women. Apparently, she wasn't the only one who found him attractive. She wasn't sure if she was happy about this or not.

Carolyn slapped playfully at his shoulder. "Still a charmer, I see," she said, and then her crystal blue eyes flipped to Surah, and the smile fell from her face like melted snow, the smooth lines of her jaw that Surah thought were pretty upon first sight sharpening and becoming harsh.

"And who is this you've brought with you?" Carolyn asked, her gaze traveling up from Surah's feet and to her face and back again.

Surah found herself clenching her teeth, but she smiled, and it looked real. She was very good at that. Then she realized that she and Charlie hadn't discussed the false identity that went with her false appearance, and she floundered in her mind, searching for a common name to spit out.

She needn't have worried. Charlie answered for her, his slow draw as sure and true as ever. Surah realized that he was an even better liar than she gave him credit for, and had she listened to her gut right then, and transported out of there, she might have been able to save herself a lot of trouble.

"This is Sarah Whittle. She's an acquaintance of mine," Charlie said, and looked back at Carolyn. "She needs to make some purchases."

Surah stepped into the house, careful to keep her smile in place and her nose from wrinkling.

"Good to meet you," she said, hoping that her fake common accent didn't *sound* fake.

Carolyn inclined her head, making Surah's hackles raise, if

they weren't raised already. "Sarah Whittle, huh? Never heard of you."

"She's from the Westlands," Charlie answered, stepping to the side a little and drawing Carolyn's attention back to him. That suggestive smile found her face again as her blue eyes travelled up Charlie's body.

Surah decided rather instantly that she didn't like this Carolyn.

"The Westlands you say?" Carolyn leaned her head around Charlie, looking at Surah again, and Surah finally came to the realization of what this woman was. The word sounded in her head in a distinct tone of disgust.

Witch.

"What part of the Westlands?"

Surah's smile remained in place, her shoulders relaxed, her composure held carefully intact. A geography test was nothing to her. She knew the lands and cities of her father's kingdom as well as anyone, and Charlie Redmine wasn't the only one who was a good liar.

"Mountain Home," she said, "It's a small town about an hour outside of Raven City."

Carolyn gave no indication of whether or not she knew the place, and really, Surah couldn't care less if she did or didn't. She could check a map if she wanted. Mountain Home would be there. Surah just wanted to get what they needed and get out of here, preferably to some place where she could breathe through her nose again.

Carolyn turned back to Charlie. "What're you lookin' for?" she asked.

Charlie rubbed a hand over his strong jaw. "A vial and a shading spell."

One of Carolyn's sharp eyebrows arched, and her eyes flicked back to Surah, who got the feeling that the Witch could see her through the glamour as surely as Surah could see what she was through hers. Not a common Sorceress, but a Witch who dealt in the black trade. Had circumstances not been what they were, Surah would have had Carolyn arrested. In fact, she made a mental note to do just that after this was all settled. It would be her final act as Keeper. She hoped.

"That's gonna run you a pretty penny," Carolyn said, flashing teeth that were too white and too straight. "You got that kinda money? This ain't a charity house I'm runnin'."

Surah nodded once. "I can pay."

"Of course you can," Carolyn said, and Surah didn't know what to think of that.

Charlie didn't shift his feet or adopt an uneasy look, but Surah got the impression that this made him tense nonetheless, or maybe it was because it made *her* tense.

"How much?" Charlie asked.

The Witch waved her hand, long fingers with the tips painted that blood-red stirring the unpleasant air, and glided over to the wall, where a shelf holding empty glass vials hung. She scanned the items and selected one. Then she moved to the shelf beside it and selected another vial containing a dark purple mixture.

Her back still to them, she said, "Not too high a price for a princess, I suspect."

Surah's heart stopped in her chest. Carolyn turned her head and looked at her over her shoulder, a smirk pulling up one corner of her pink-painted lips, crystal blue eyes glittering with mischief. Surah dropped her Glamour, her hair going lavender and her cloak reverting back to the black that shimmered when it caught the light. She raised her chin a fraction, almost relieved to shed the pretense.

"You know me, then, Witch," she said, it was not a question, nor a compliment.

Carolyn laughed, the sound crawling up Surah's spine rather than ringing in her ears. "Everyone knows you, *princess,"* she replied, making the address sound as dirty as Surah's had.

Surah looked at Charlie, hoping her undeniable disappointment didn't show on her face. But he looked as surprised at this revelation as she felt, and that one moment of her furrowing her eyebrows in confusion was the last moment that she could have possibly made her escape. And maybe escaped her fate as well.

The voice came from the open doorway, which Surah had left ajar to vent some of the putrid smell in the dark cottage. She heard it at the same moment that the dark power washed over her, at the same moment as she felt the necklace holding her royal stone snap and fly free of her neck. Her hand reached up to catch it, her breath catching in her throat as well, but she missed, the chain just narrowly evading her fingers, and it was too late.

She spun on her heels, cloak fluttering around her in a quiet swish, and there stood Black Heart.

Her royal stone rested in the palm of his gloved hand. Surah considered trying to make a grab for it, but Black Heart closed his fingers around the stone and smiled the way one might at a naughty child. Surah's gut clenched as she looked into his face and saw that his eyes were the exact same emerald color as Charlie's.

"Let's not be hasty," Black Heart said. He offered Surah a small bow. She was struck speechless.

The instinct to snap her fingers and portal out of here came, but she cursed in her head when she realized she would need her stone to do this. The next realization that came was even worse. Black Heart was blocking the door. The Black Stone, much larger than she expected, hung around his neck, pulsing that sickening dark power that seemed to fill the room even more fully than the awful smell of the Witch's home. She was trapped.

Charlie Redmine had set her up. Somehow, though she

knew this was completely insane, this realization was the worst of all.

When a familiar voice spoke in her head, Surah's knees nearly went lax with relief. In all the shock she had forgotten about Samson, who was slinking around the house just outside the door.

"Can I kill him, love?"

Surah couldn't stop her eyes from flicking to Charlie, who had a very peculiar look on his face, as if he was as taken off guard by all this as she was. She wasn't fooled. Charlie Redmine was an extraordinary actor.

"Yes," she told Samson silently.

"You ought to tell that beast of yours to back up," Black Heart said, his voice deep and gleeful. He wrapped his hand around the Black Stone, thick fingers barely covering the surface. "Unless you fancy yourself a dead tiger and a severed throat."

Hot, red anger welled up in Surah now, and her fists clenched at her sides, but she said nothing. She could tell by Black Heart's hard expression that he would do exactly as he promised if she made a false move, and it would be all too easy with the Black Stone in his hand. Even if she still had her small piece of the White Stone, she would be no match to the power that he had stolen.

The fact that she wasn't dead already gave her a dash of hope, but it was just a dash. She told Samson silently to stand back, and the tiger retreated into the grasses a bit with barely contained rage.

Surah's heart was tripping, but she inclined her head, holding Black Heart's gaze with concealed effort. "If you wanted to kill me, you would have already done so," she said her soft voice clear and strong. "So what is it you want?"

Black Heart smiled. He had an ugly smile, nothing like his brother's, who hadn't said a word at this new arrival. Carolyn stood over by Charlie, just as silent, but with a very pleased look on her face. Surah didn't see what either of their expressions were, though, because she thought that taking her gaze away from Black Heart for even a moment would be a very stupid idea.

This was the first time she'd encountered the man other than when he'd busted his brother out of the holding cell, but she could see why he'd gained the reputation he had. Darkness seemed as much a part of him as shadows are part of the night.

"I do want to kill you, princess," Black Heart said, and his pleasant tone did not at all match the words. "Just not quite yet. I want to kill both you and your father…How is he by the way?"

Now the anger Surah felt turned into fury, something that she could feel in her bones and taste in her mouth. Her next words came out of her mouth quickly, and she made no effort to stop them.

"Not concerning himself with the piddling of common cowards," she said.

Black Heart struck out so fast that even if Surah had known what was coming, she probably wouldn't have been able to avoid it. The knuckles on the back of his hand connected with the side of her cheek so hard that a few stars burst behind her eyes, and the cracking sound it made resounded like thunder in the tiny room, drowning out the sounds of breathing and racing hearts.

Pain exploded on the left side of her face; immediate and harsh and terrible, making her eyes water and her back hot. Her head was whipped to the side, wrenching her neck.

Surah did not cry out. She didn't make a sound.

She reached up and touched her lip, seeing a spot of blood on her gloved finger, and met Black Heart's emerald eyes with a death promise clear on the surface of her violet ones. Her face still hurt, was rippling with pain and heat, but her lips pulled up in a small smile.

She refused to look over at Charlie, so she didn't see the barely concealed fury on his own face. She just stared at Black Heart, thinking that if he had any brains at all, he would kill her now, because if she were going to live through this, she would see to it that *he* wouldn't.

Samson was coming now, she could practically feel the heat of his anger across the distance between them, and she told him very sternly to stand down. Black Heart could do any number of things with that Stone around his neck, and Surah would not be able to contain herself if something happened to Sam.

Attacking Black Heart right now was a sure way to get them both killed. The man obviously had no boundaries, and Surah could be a very patient person.

She pushed her chin out, ignoring the blood that trickled over her lip, her voice strong and steady, royal. "Feel better?" she asked.

Black Heart laughed heartily, the stone around his neck bouncing a little on his wide chest. He ran a hand through his hair, which was slicked back into a tight ponytail. He came forward and gripped Surah's shoulder, his touch rough and slightly painful.

"Much better, princess," he said, giving her that toothy smile. "Thank you for asking. Now if you've nothing left to add, let us be on our way. There is so much to be done."

He turned to the others. "Thank you for your help, Carolyn."

The Witch nodded, batting those black eyelashes and smiling that pink smile. Black Heart looked at Charlie and jerked his head. "Come, little brother," he said, extending his free hand to him. "You've done well."

Charlie came over to them, his movements robotic, as if he was being controlled with magic by his brother. "I didn't know," he told her. "I didn't have any part of this."

Surah finally looked at Charlie as he came to a stop in front of her. She didn't believe a word he said. She wouldn't make that mistake again.

"Surah," Charlie said, "I swear it. I didn't know he'd be here."

Surah pulled her eyes away a moment before Black Heart pushed them through a portal to wherever he had in mind, and her last thought was one that she would never—*if* she lived through this—ever forget.

I gave you an inch, and you took way more than a mile.

19

SURAH

Black Heart still had hold of Surah's shoulder, and she yanked herself away from him and delicately smoothed out her cloak, returning his annoyed stare defiantly.

He may have taken her captive, and he may be planning to kill her, but she did have her pride, and right now, it was getting the best of her.

Surprisingly, it was anger that was fueling her, rather than the fear she certainly should be feeling. It took her a moment to realize she was angrier with Charlie Redmine than she was afraid of his brother.

At least, for the moment. That would change very shortly.

Surah jerked a little as her hands clasped in front of her without a signal from her brain to do so, and smoky black handcuffs enclosed her wrists, making an immovable figure eight there. Black Heart released hold of the stone at his throat and smiled as Surah tested the strength of her dark magical bonds.

"I assure you they are quite solid, princess," he said.

Surah returned his smirk, forcibly ignoring Charlie as if he weren't even there.

"Of course," she said, her voice smooth and calm. Inside, her heart was threatening to rip through her ribcage.

They were in the jungle. Likely the Southlands jungle; the most dangerous of the four. The trees were thick and green, crawling with vines and bursting with colorful plants. She could hear the sound of a waterfall in the distance, the call of birds and the rustling of smaller animals. The sunlight peeking through the lush canopy shifted down in glittering, golden streams, the thickness of the brush surely hiding much greater beasts.

Black Heart leaned into her now, his neck craning down and his hot breath pushing into her face. He towered over her. Surah met his eyes and refused to flinch. Next to them, though the princess didn't see it, Charlie tensed.

"Don't be scared, princess," Black Heart said, his voice pitched low and falsely gentle. He patted the Stone around his neck with his right hand. "The beasts wouldn't dare attack while I have this. Come now." He gave her a rough push forward. "Let's get moving."

Surah walked, her back straight and head high and heart low. She couldn't believe she was in this situation, couldn't believe she had been so stupid as to trust a man like Charlie Redmine, with his handsome face and calm manner and blunt, inappropriate way of talking. She should have killed him in her bedroom, as soon as she set eyes on him. Or let Theo kill him.

Now, she was in the middle of the Southland jungle with a crazed Sorcerer and Samson wasn't here and her stone was gone and her father was dying. All because she'd given an inch. If she lived through this, she was going to literally punch Sam in the nose for that terrible advice.

The two men walked behind her, their heavy shoes making the vegetation crunch underfoot. Surah kept ahead of them and concentrated on two things; keeping her calm, and making sure she lived long enough to see the two of them punished. It was a savage part of her that had been cultivated over the years, a strong survival instinct that had saved her on more than one occasion. The ability to shut out her emotions and be pragmatic was key right now.

Theo would be looking for her, as would her father, if he was even physically able. So would Samson. She just had to wait for her moment to escape, and seize it when it came. Easy.

She swallowed. She hated Charlie Redmine and his crazy brother. She *hated* them.

They walked for a little ways through the trees, the sound of the waterfall in the distance growing closer and closer until at last they reached the source. The cliff from which the water poured over was small, only fifteen feet high or so. It spilled into a small river that shimmered in the sunlight, reflecting the images of the trees leaning out over it. The rushing of the water filled Surah's head, and she was glad when it drowned out the sound of the blood rushing in her ears.

When Surah came to a stop Black Heart reached out to push her forward again, but before he could, Charlie snatched up his wrist in a hard grip and met his brother's eyes with a level stare.

Black Heart smiled innocently, and Charlie released his hold slowly. "You won't touch her again," Charlie said. "I won't let you."

Surah narrowed her eyes on him.

Black Heart only grinned and stepped around Surah. His movements were lithe and graceful as he moved toward the edge of the waterfall, where large gray rocks jutted out over the lake. He hopped onto the nearest one, the mist of water clinging to his black cloak in tiny droplets, and extended his hand to Surah, smiling.

"Come, princess. Watch your step."

Surah, her hands still bound in front of her, leapt onto the rock gracefully, not at all tottering for balance, ignoring the offered assistance. Black Heart laughed again and clapped his hands. Charlie followed behind her, and Surah resisted the urge to shove him over the edge and into the river, where maybe he would drown.

The string of obscenities running through her head in that moment would have put her lost mother to shame.

Black Heart led them into a small cave behind the waterfall, which was dark and damp and cool. He cast a small light sphere, which illuminated the place just enough to see by. Then he turned and faced them.

"Have a seat, princess. Make yourself comfortable."

Surah felt her knees give way and was forced to the ground under an invisible weight. Black tendrils of smoke rose from the floor and looped around the dark cuffs encircling her wrists, chaining her to the earth and making a lump form in her throat.

Now the fear came, and it was all she could do to keep the tears from forming in her eyes. She refused to let them see her cry. She raised her chin and straightened her back as much as she could with her wrists chained to the floor.

"Comfortable?" Black Heart asked.

Surah glared up at him. "Very," she said.

Black Heart clasped his hands in front of him and settled down to the floor in front of her. Charlie stood off to the side, silent.

"Wonderful," Black Heart said. "We wouldn't want our princess to be uncomfortable."

Surah just looked at him.

He ran a hand over the slicked-back ponytail on his head, arranged his cloak beneath him. "First," he said, "let me apologize for this." He reached up to touch Surah's face, which was starting to darken to a deep purple where he had struck her. Surah jerked her head away from his fingers. Black Heart sighed. "I don't believe in hitting women," he said.

Surah's teeth clenched. "Yes, that much is clear."

Black Heart laughed. "You've got spunk," he said. "I'll give you that, but it would behoove you to cooperate with me, princess."

Surah said nothing.

"I just have a few questions to ask you, and if you answer them, this will all be quick and painless. Time is of the essence, as I'm sure you're aware."

Silence.

"What happened to your brother?"

This question was not what Surah had been expecting, but she was sure to keep the surprise free of her face. She pressed her lips together, held her tongue.

"He was murdered by the King of Vampires and Wolves, was he not?"

Surah said nothing.

"And your father, did he seek revenge for Syris's death?"

Surah inclined her head a fraction, held his gaze, and said nothing.

Black Heart sighed. "You're not in the talking mood." He reached into his cloak and pulled out a silver sundial, flicked open the face, glanced down at it, looked back up at her. "Your father probably has all of thirty-six hours left to live." He stood, towering over Surah like a pillar of black stone. "Perhaps twenty hours here will loosen your tongue."

Surah looked up at him, said nothing.

Black Heart's returning smile made her teeth clench, and she had to ball her bound hands into fists to keep them from shaking.

"I'll see you soon, princess," he said, and turned on his heels. He looked at Charlie. "He wasn't lying, by the way. Charlie didn't know I'd be at the Witches place, but I know him, and I knew he'd go." He winked at Surah and turned toward the mouth of the cave. "Come, brother, let us have a discussion." Then he stepped out of the cave and beneath the waterfall.

Charlie was yanked forward, as if he were being pulled by a

magical leash, but Surah pointedly avoided his gaze. His voice was low and deep and sad when he spoke. "I'm sorry, princess," he said.

She looked at him now, her purple eyes burning as the clock of her father's life ticked down.

"No, Charlie," she said. "Not yet, you aren't."

20

KING SYRIAN

King Syrian was in bed when the message came. He had been bed-ridden for the past few hours, having told the servants to make sure no one bothered him. He didn't want anyone to see him in the state he was in, which was, to say the least, terrible.

He was running a fever and all the muscles in his body hurt. It was as if he could feel the poison spreading through him, entering his bloodstream and making him weak. His head pounded, the dim light in the room making even his eyes ache. In all his years he couldn't remember ever feeling so awful.

And it was just getting worse.

The clock was ticking. He could practically hear it counting down the seconds of his life in the silence of his bedroom. What was worse, Theo said that Surah was missing, and he hadn't heard from her in several hours. He cursed his weakness as he lie there, wishing he was strong enough to go out and look for Surah himself.

He wasn't quite panicked yet. Surah was a smart girl, a great fighter and well-trained in the magics. He took comfort in this, and knew she could probably look after herself. In fact, chances were that she was just out looking for a way to cure him, and he could just picture her raising her chin and giving him that sweet smile, so much like her mother's, when he told her how worried he'd been.

Then the message came, and the fear and panic and dread came with it.

His eyes were closed when it happened, but he opened them when the world beyond his lids shadowed, like a cloud passing over the sun on a bright day.

He lifted his head, then pulled himself into a painful sitting position, staring at the black smoke that was swirling in front of him, the source of the darkness that had fallen over the room. His eyes narrowed down to slits as he realized what it was.

A message, sent with black magic.

The smoke swirled and danced and finally settled into a black rectangle, like the frame of a picture. In the center of the frame, Black Heart's face took stage. Syrian knew the message was recorded, and that Black Heart could not hear him, but he uttered a string of obscenities that burned his poor throat.

The face in the picture smiled. "Syrian," It began, the voice gleeful and menacing. "How are you, dearest king?" A deep laugh. "Not so well? That's most unfortunate. But I am so pleased to finally have your attention. I suppose I should have just gone after your precious Highborn ladies years ago. You wouldn't have disregarded me then. But that's all in the past, right? There are more important matters to consider now, and I think you will be a wonderful listener this time. That is, if your old ears are still up to hearing."

Another laugh. King Syrian tightened his hands into hard fists in his lap. It made his fingers ache.

The recorded message continued. "My demands are simple, and though I shouldn't have to explain them to you, I will, because I am well aware that you can be a...slow learner. First, you will renounce the throne to the kingdom and name me,

Michael Redmine, king. Then, you will hand over the White Stone and all of its accompanying pieces."

A pause. Now King Syrian was the one who laughed. It shook painfully in his chest.

"You will do these things for two reasons," Black Heart continued. "The first reason is because it is the right thing to do. You are old and weak. Your rein has run its course, and our people are in need of a capable leader in the dark times ahead. I will be that leader. I will protect those who you would disregard, the same way you disregarded them in the war not so long ago. The common people will stand behind me, and embrace the new way of life, because they too know you are weak."

Another pause. King Syrian rolled his eyes a little. Black Heart had always been a fanatic, and he would get nothing. Except what all murderers and traitors to the kingdom got, and it certainly wasn't the throne.

"And the second reason, in case you are not thus far convinced, my brave King, is because you are going to die anyway. No matter if you meet my demands or not. You will die. The only thing you can hope to do now is save your precious daughter from the same fate. She's a lovely woman, by the way. Such manners!"

Now Syrian's heart raced, his already sweaty back and neck springing fresh salt water from the pores, the room going instantly hot. Some of the pain rushed away from his body and he sprung up from the bed, exhilaration taking its place.

Then, the strength left him again, sliding away as though it had never been, and he fell forward and landed back on the bed.

Black Heart's recording continued on, as if it had been allowing for just such reaction. "I have her, Syrian. I have your daughter stashed away nice and cozy, but she won't remain that way for long. You can waste what little time I am going to give you checking to see if I'm telling the truth, or you can just believe me and start contemplating your decision. As far as how much time she has…let's just say it is even less than you do, my king, and in my experience, demon poison can be quite expedient. Have a good day, my Liege. It is, after all, one of your last."

Then the smoke vanished, taking with it the face of the man who claimed to have his daughter. King Syrian was beside himself, unable to process what was happening. It was a terribly paralyzing moment, because he was usually such a self-controlled man. So much had happened over the years, so many that he loved gone, so much lost. He wasn't sure he could bear to lose his last child, not his little Surah, too. It was unthinkable. It made him almost long for the death that was slowly taking him.

He fell back on the bed and stared up at the ceiling, the pain of his condition coming back to him in full force. He couldn't breathe. He rubbed a hand over his eyes, brushing away a single hot tear. He felt very common in that moment, not kingly or royal or even worthy. Then the anger came to him, his longtime enemy and savior, and it rushed through his body in a welcome wave.

He straightened himself up in bed with agonizing effort, gritting his teeth against groans of pain. When he was upright, he smoothed a hand through his hair and down his silk robe, brushing the moisture from his head with the sleeve of his arm. He snapped his fingers, and the door to his room swung open. One of the Hunters standing guard stepped around the corner.

"Yes, my liege?"

Syrian suppressed a cough, cleared his throat. "Summon Theodine Gray," he ordered, and rested his head back against the high headboard of the bed, swallowing to keep back more bloody coughs.

A few minutes later, the Head Hunter entered the room, sweeping in gracefully, his cloak flowing behind him. He bowed. "What can I do for you, my liege?"

"My daughter, has she returned?"

Theo shook his head, gray eyes taking in Syrian's condition. "No, my liege."

"How long has she been gone?"

"Nearly three hours," Theo said, as if he'd been counting the minutes.

Syrian met his eyes, his voice sounding stronger than he felt. "And you've looked for her, I assume."

Theo nodded.

"Black Heart claims he has her."

Syrian watched as Theo absorbed this information, saw the tightening of his jaw and the clenching of his fists, glad to see that the Head Hunter cared for his daughter so much, since someone strong would be needed if they had a hope of finding her.

He honestly couldn't understand Surah's hesitation over marrying Theodine Gray. He would make a good husband, a good king, which may be likely to be sooner than Syrian had planned for. And which was of no matter right now.

"He sent a message?" Theo asked, his tone low and angry.

Syrian nodded slowly, his neck aching, regarding Theo through blurry eyes. A cough racked his chest, a deep, nasty rattling that was unstoppable. He snatched a handkerchief from the bedside table, too weak to even use his magic to summon one. It went to his mouth white and came away red.

When the fit passed, Syrian said, "You love my daughter, Hunter Gray, do you not?"

Theo's response was immediate. "With all my heart, my liege."

Syrian nodded once more. "Then find her." He coughed again, this one lasting longer, his entire body jerking with the force. When he finally regained control over himself, he looked gravely at the Head Hunter.

"Find her and save her. Kill this man who has dared to take her prisoner and threatened the kingdom. Kill Black Heart and his brother and anyone else who would stand beside them." Syrian stared at him, and knowing that Theo had never seen his king as desperate as he was now.

"Do this for me, Theo," he continued, "and you have my blessing to marry my daughter. I will make the announcement myself, assuming I am still able."

Theodine Gray bowed low to his king, concealing the small, crooked smile on his face. "With pleasure, my liege."

21

SURAH

Surah crossed her legs beneath her, trying to find a way to sit that wouldn't hurt her wrists so much. Each time she shifted in the slightest, the dark bonds encircling her wrists tightened, and they were so constricted now that they pulsed. Her fingers were beginning to go numb.

The sound of the water rushing over the rocks was loud and constant and irritating, but did nothing to drown out the rapid beating of her heart. The moisture in the small cave was as thick as a sauna. She wished she could have removed her cloak, because the temperature seemed to be rising and rising as the day wore on.

Or maybe it was just that her panic and fear were starting to overtake her. She had to calm herself and think.

She looked all around the dark cavern, grateful that at least Black Heart had left the little light sphere ablaze for her to see by. She had no idea what she was looking for, even though she knew she wouldn't find it. It's not like he would have left some magical key to the handcuffs lying around for her to find and slowly drag toward her with the heel of her boot. This thought made her laugh, but it sounded forced even to her own ears.

She didn't hear his return, was too busy staring down at her bound hands and trying to gain control over her racing thoughts, but when she looked up again, he was there, and she breathed a mental sigh of relief to see that it was Charlie and not Black Heart, then chastised herself for doing so.

Charlie Redmine was just as dangerous as his brother, probably more so. She would not make the mistake of forgetting that.

She stared at him a moment because there was nothing else to be done and because she couldn't help it. He had his old guitar in his hand, holding it at his side by the neck. His handsome face was blank and guarded, but his emerald eyes betrayed some inner roiling. Surah jerked her gaze away.

Lying eyes, those were.

He said nothing as he entered the cave, just went over to the rock wall and leaned against it, sliding down to a seated position with his long legs sprawled out in front of him, gently positioning the guitar in his lap. Surah could feel his eyes on her, but she refused to look at him again. He didn't deserve her attention.

When his hands began to stroke the strings, soft soothing notes coming together to make a lulling rhythm, Surah did look up, and her anger came rushing back to her in a hot wave.

"Stop that," she snapped.

Charlie's fingers halted at once and his eyes flicked up to meet hers. "All right," he said.

This response served only to anger her more. "How long have you and your brother been planning this?"

Charlie just looked at her.

Surah gritted her teeth, her usually sweet voice edged with anger. "So you're just going to ignore me? You don't think I deserve to at least know the answers to my questions before your brother murders me? Or is that what *you're* here for?"

She couldn't be sure, but she thought she saw Charlie flinch.

Silence hung for a moment. Then, he said, "That's not gonna happen, princess."

Surah laughed. "Is that so? You could've fooled me."

Charlie said nothing, just looked at her underneath dark lashes.

Surah tried to throw her hands up, and winced when the cuffs tightened again and realized she couldn't. "That's all you have to say?"

Charlie shrugged. "I try not to say anything when I know I won't be heard."

"You're a true gentleman, Mr. Redmine. You know that?"

Charlie set the guitar gently on the ground and folded his hands in his lap. "All right," he said. "You got any ideas, then?"

Surah laughed again, and the harsh sound of it reminded her that she was losing her composure. She pulled it back to her with some effort. "Oh, I have plenty of ideas. I just don't think you or your crazy brother would go for them."

Charlie sighed and rubbed a hand over his jaw. "Try me."

Surah's brow furrowed. What in the world was going on with this man? His words didn't match his actions and his actions never matched the emotions hidden behind his eyes. For a moment, she couldn't think of anything to say.

"What are you talking about?" she asked.

Charlie gestured to the black chains around her wrists. "Got any ideas on how to break those?"

Surah looked down at the cuffs and back up at Charlie, her eyebrows still furrowed in confusion. "Why would you want to do that?"

Charlie pulled his knees up and rested his arms over them, rolling his neck slowly so that his dark hair fell into his face a little. Then he looked up at her, and Surah hated herself for again thinking how attractive he was.

"Because whether you believe it or not, I didn't want any of this to happen. I had nothing to do with it, just like my brother said. He's left for now and he knows I won't leave this place without you, but he'll be back, and we need to not be here when he returns."

Surah just looked at him, the disbelief evident on her face.

"And," he continued, his voice dropping a fraction, "I have no intention of letting Michael hurt you again. I could've killed him just for hitting you the first time."

"Really? Well, you'll forgive me for calling bullshit on that one."

Charlie shrugged, held up his hands, as if to say "*See.*"

"Why is that, Mr. Redmine? Because you are so loyal to the kingdom that you would betray your own brother?"

He was silent a moment. Then, he shook his head. "Not to the kingdom."

It took Surah longer than it should have to recognize the implication there. When she did, she tried to force it away, knew that it would be foolish to believe it, but a little hope spiraled in her chest nonetheless.

"Then why did you take me to that Witch's house?" she asked, not liking that her voice came out smaller than she intended.

Charlie shook his head, as if he wondered the same thing himself. "I should have known better," he said. "I'm sorry about that. This is my fault."

"That's the first honest thing you've said since we met."

"No, it's not."

Surah tried to throw up her hands again. The cuffs tightened. She winced.

"Stop doing that."

"Then stop saying things to irritate me," she snapped.

Charlie rubbed a hand down his jaw again. "Look, we can sit here and argue until my brother gets back, or you can start telling me how those chains can be broken. You've got to get a hold of your emotions and think, Surah, because I don't have the slightest clue how to help you. All magic can be broken, right? So…how?"

"Stop calling me that."

Charlie sighed.

Surah stared at him, her mind flying a mile a minute. She knew she couldn't trust him, but what choice did she have? No one was going to find her in time, and her father was as good as dead if she didn't find a way out of here. She was as good as dead, too. She bit her lip, tasting the blood there from when Black Heart had struck her, and tried to think.

Charlie was right, all magic could be broken, just like the demon poisoning could be cured with the Black Stone. So there had to be a way to break these bonds. She was sure she had read about just such a thing in her studies at some point, but could not recall any specifics.

But she knew someone who might know a way. It was a long shot, but it was all she had.

"Bassil," she said.

"What?"

"Bassil, the Warlock who works at my father's castle. He might know a way."

Charlie straightened up and leaned forward, emerald eyes intense. "How do I get to him?"

Surah's eyes flicked to him, and she hated that his very serious expression caused more hope to spiral in her. "Do you still have the piece of Black Stone your brother gave you?"

Charlie nodded. He reached into the pocket of his flannel shirt and pulled out two items. Surah gasped and her heart nearly stopped when she saw what they were.

"How did you get those?"

Charlie smiled, the small quirk of his lips making heat pulse in her midsection in spite of herself. "I took them from Carolyn's," he said. "Thought they might come in handy."

Surah stared at the stone vial and other one with a dark

purple liquid inside—a shading spell. The stone vial could be used to capture power from the Black Stone, enough with which to save her father, and the shading spell was for invisibility. Surah was so relieved she thought she could kiss Charlie Redmine. Then she remembered how ridiculous that was and shoved the thought away.

"They could help," she said.

Charlie stood, his movements smooth and graceful, and came over to Surah, kneeling down in front of her. She could smell the clean scent of him, which was like rain and pine and sunlight blown to her by a warm breeze. His handsome face was level with her own, his bright eyes standing out like gems in the darkness of the cave.

"Tell me what to do, princess," he said, the slow drawl of his voice somehow very intimate in the small space.

Surah found that she had to swallow before she could speak. Twice. Her voice came out low and husky, almost a whisper.

"You have to go to the castle and find Bassil. Explain to him the situation. He will help you…if he believes you're telling the truth."

"No trouble there."

Surah found a smile trying to touch her lips, but stopped it before it could make an appearance. "Of course not," she said.

One side of Charlie's mouth pulled up. "I'll be back as soon as I can," he said, and then, as if he just couldn't help himself, he reached up and brushed back a lavender curl that had fallen forward on her face, covering the purple bruise where Black Heart had struck her. His fingertips were calloused but gentle, running lightly over her soft skin, making her shiver in spite of herself.

"This won't happen again," he added, voice low and deep, studying the bruise with what Surah thought was concealed anger and something else she didn't care to contemplate. "You have my word on that, princess."

Surah's heart did a flip. There was nothing she could do to stop it.

"Okay," she said.

Charlie's hand lingered by her face for a moment, then he stood to go. Surah called out to him before he slipped beneath the waterfall.

"Charlie?" she said.

He turned back to face her.

Her voice was small and soft and completely unguarded when she spoke. She didn't hate it as much as she thought she would, as much as she probably *should*. It was almost liberating to speak so truly.

"I really hope you're not lying."

Charlie smiled, and she hated that it was impossible to hate him when he did so.

"I'm not, princess," he said. "I'm not."

2 2

———

SAMSON

$\mathscr{H}$e was exhausted. Pain-in-his-side, panting-for-breath exhausted. He was not built to run very long distances, more so for short, quick bursts of speed, but he could not stop. No matter how tired and hungry and thirsty he was, he could not stop.

He was headed for the jungle to the south of the kingdom, and he still had a good distance to go. Time was his greatest enemy right now, because time was also hers. Who knew what that man could be doing to her? The thought made fury burn in his chest.

Samson held his head low as he crossed the grasslands, his powerful legs propelling him forward. The scents of the land assaulting his nose; pollen and pine and wild honeysuckle and so on. The sunlight beamed down on him harshly and made his eyes slit to half-mast. This was not the ideal way to spend an afternoon. He much preferred napping.

But Surah needed him. Now more than ever before, she needed him. He had no doubt in his mind that the man who called himself Black Heart would kill her; *if* he hadn't done it already. How badly Samson had wanted to rip his throat out back in that Witch's rank cabin. How badly he'd wanted to kill them all. Black Heart and the Witch and Charlie Redmine, that deceitful bastard. He could practically taste the tang of their blood on his tongue now.

He couldn't believe he'd told Surah to give that man an inch. He couldn't believe his instincts were wrong about Charlie. He'd known upon first smell of that cottage that darkness lived inside. He could smell it on Black Heart as soon as he'd appeared, all the way from the field behind the cottage.

But Charlie Redmine hadn't been like them. He'd been almost an exact opposite, actually, all calm waters, where the other two were raging seas. Samson couldn't ever remember being so wrong about someone before.

Now he had to fix it. And he would. They would pay for every hair harmed on the princess's head in flesh and blood. As far as Samson was concerned, they were dead men walking.

He stopped only once because he had to, at a small river about halfway to his destination. He not only drank the water, but waded into it, letting it cool his hot fur and soothe his parched throat. Then he was on his way again, racing under the sun with wide strides and a heaving chest.

When he came to the edge of the Southlands jungle, he nearly collapsed into the shade of the thick green trees. His tongue felt like a very large, dry sponge in his mouth. His eyes were wind-burned and his jaws agape as he sucked in painful air. He knew he needed to hurry, but he also knew it would be a death wish to head any further into the jungle in such a weak state.

So he slept. Well, he napped. Only for twenty minutes or so. He just lay there, on the edge of the jungle, in the partial shade of the trees, his eyes closed and his troubled mind letting go for a moment. Then he was up again. Rested and ready to move to the next necessities. More water. And food.

And precious time was ticking away. But he couldn't very

well help her if he was dead. Also, he was resourceful. He could probably kill two birds with one stone. But, first, the water.

His head lifted as he tested the air, searching for the scent of moisture. He found it and followed its trail, his ears perked, amber eyes watchful as he passed beneath the trees.

He could feel them out there, the other beasts, watching him, their own heads surely cocking or tilting as his smell found them on the breeze. It made a rush of exhilaration fill him, his heart kicking up in speed. He was already fantasizing about the hunt ahead.

Nothing attacked him, and he made it to the source of the water, which was little more than a stream running over a bed of jagged rocks, one he could easily hop over. He lowered his head to the edge and drank for a long time, until his belly sloshed inside when he moved. When he was finished he looked all around, trying to figure the quickest route to complete his task.

He had heard Surah say that the Black Stone was in this jungle, after the tracking spell she'd performed with Bassil using the eagle's blood. The Southlands jungle was the second smallest of the eight, and also the jungle where he'd been born and raised before Surah had found him.

It was just a patch on the map compared to most of the others, but if he was going to hold someone prisoner, this is where he would come. It was a good distance from the city, and also had the most hidden caverns and small caves. You could hide someone in one of those small spaces for an eternity and not have them found.

If he had a hope of finding Surah in time, he would need to speak to the beast king in this land, and there was a whole history between them that was sure to complicate things.

Well, he had to find him first.

Samson lowered his head between his shoulders, his body slinking low to the ground. He found the trail of a female panther and followed it, his paws moving silently over the earth. High above him, great birds called out to the open skies, serpents wound around branches, and primates sat atop limbs. The canopy was a thick, impermeable green, only traces of sunlight forcing through. The ground was soft with moisture, the air free of the smells of men. Sometimes Samson longed to roam free again, to prowl the jungles, stalking at night, hunting and eating and sleeping on low tree limbs during the day, letting the sunlight sink into his fur, letting his instincts rule him.

But he had given that all up, and would do so again, for her. She had given him a greater purpose in life, one he wouldn't have ever known existed. She had given him love. He simply could not fathom a life without her.

He stopped when he heard the female panther up ahead, only twenty feet or so southwest, downwind. She was a young one, by the smell of her, and in the middle of a hunt. He could smell the trail masked beneath her own, that of a buck. His eyes narrowed as he smiled inside, thinking of how right he was about two birds and one stone. This was almost too easy.

The female panther broke her cover, charging ahead. Samson followed and watched as she leapt into the air, the buck realizing she was there just a moment too late and trying to break into a run.

The black panther landed on its back, square between the buck's shoulders, powerful jaws sinking into the meaty flesh of its neck, claws digging deeply into the hide for purchase. The buck reared, sharp antler's slashing the air as its eyes went wide with terror. It ran thirty feet or so and fell to the ground, blood seeping down its neck where the female was busy ripping and tearing, trying to get at the throat without being snagged by those deadly antlers.

Samson watched from the sidelines, his blood rushing in his ears, his heart racing like a prize horse. He watched and waited.

Slowly, the buck ceased its fighting, one dead eye staring heavenward where it lay on its side.

The female dismounted her kill, her midnight coat as black as oil. She delicately licked the blood from her face, then moved in to claim her prize.

Samson moved forward.

She was mid-bite when she saw him step through the trees, and a low growl issued from her throat, her eyes locked on his. She was smaller than Samson, of course, but not by too much, standing nearly six feet tall from head to paw. Her head lowered and her slim legs coiled, determined to keep her kill.

Samson couldn't help an internal chuckle. The female was no match for him, and they both knew it.

Her voice sounded in his head, a husky, deep growl riding the words.

"Get your own, tiger."

Samson took a few steps forward, amber eyes locked on hers. *"I think not, panther."*

He rushed forward, jaws wide and snapping, slashing at her with his sharp claws. The female snapped and slashed as well, but she back-pedaled, nearly tripping over her prey in her escape.

Samson stood over the buck, his head still low, daring her with his eyes to try and take the kill back from him. When she just stood there, her black chest heaving with anger, he bent down and tore at the flesh of the buck with his teeth, swallowing large chunks of raw, bloody meat.

The female stood watching him. *"You fool,"* she growled. *"You have no idea who I am, do you?"*

Samson continued eating, flicking her a look that said he couldn't care less.

The panther narrowed her silver eyes. *"My father is king in these lands, and he will have you killed for this. I will taste your flesh by nightfall."*

Samson lifted his head, really looking at her for the first time. He saw now what he should have seen before. The silver of her eyes, the scar on her left flank, the arrogant tilt of her head. He wasn't sure how he'd missed it in her scent, but he could smell it now. His rough tongue ran out slowly over his lips as he tried to jumpstart what were suddenly his frozen thoughts. It had been over a decade since he'd last seen her, since that day when Surah had saved him from the serpent and claimed him for her own.

"Mila?"

The panther's head tilted, her eyes narrowing. *"Who are you?"* she asked.

He stepped back from the buck, which was a mess of entrails and torn flesh, his eyes on her. Her defensive posture relaxed as she raised her head to her full height. The angry growl was gone from her voice when she spoke again in his head.

"Sam?"

Samson lifted his head in a nod.

"I thought you were dead."

"I almost was."

She was silent for a moment, as if she just couldn't believe it.

"Where have you been all this time?" She asked, and Samson felt a little guilt spiral in him at the slight hurt in her tone.

He was almost ashamed to answer. *"Living with a Sorceress."*

She took a step forward. *"You were captured?"*

"No."

She paused. *"What do you mean, no?"*

Samson sighed internally. There was no way to explain this that she would understand. Beasts, as a rule, did not live among people. They certainly didn't leave the jungles to be with them. He didn't even have time to begin to explain Surah to Mila. Surah didn't have time.

"The day the serpent attacked us, when we were both cubs, you remember?"

Mila gave him a look that said that was a stupid question.

Samson continued on. *"I tried to fight the thing, and sent you off to find help."*

"I know, and when I got back with help, you were gone. I thought you were dead, digested by that snake and being shit out somewhere. You think I would have forgotten? What does that have to do with living with a Sorceress?"

Samson could tell she was angry, and he couldn't blame her. He remembered now how vulgar she could be when she was angry, so different from Surah with her constant composure. It brought back many memories he didn't care to think of.

"I would have been dead. But a Sorceress saved me," he explained. *"She subdued the serpent and took me to safety, and I...stayed with her."*

For a moment, Mila was silent. Then her voice took on that growl again in his head. *"You* stayed with her? *Everyone thought you were gone. We held a ceremony in your name. Your mother cried in front of both of our families... I cried."*

Samson's gut twisted, but he ignored it. She had every right to feel this way, but it wasn't like he could do anything about it now. But he was going to need her help, and if he had learned anything about females from living with Surah for so long, it was that you caught a lot more bees if you used honey.

"I'm sorry, Mila."

Mila let out a loud growl that reverberated between the trees. *"You're sorry? That's all you have to say? You're sorry?"* She turned around and began heading through the trees, her muscular shoulders stiff, her tail held still. *"You're sorry doesn't mean shit to me. Enjoy the buck, traitor."*

Samson sighed. Surah was lucky he loved her. He would not have come home to face this if he didn't. Then again, he never would have *left* home if not for her, either.

He left the downed buck and chased after Mila, catching up

to her easily. She held her head forward and refused to look at him.

Mila, please, I need your help.

Mila huffed. *"Go ask your precious Sorceress for help."*

Samson came to a stop in front of her, blocking her path. *"She can't. She's been captured, and I think she's here somewhere. The man who has her will kill her if I don't find her."*

"And why the hell should I care? I don't give a shit about two-legs, and they don't give a shit about us. Let her die."

She went to move around him. He blocked her path again. *"I can't do that, Mila. You don't understand."*

"You're right, I don't."

Samson had to suppress a growl. He didn't have time for this. Females could be so exhausting. He took a deep breath, completely unsure as to whether his next words would help his case, or hurt it. He said them anyway.

"I love her, Mila."

Mila just stared at him, unblinking. She stared at him for so long that he felt sure she was going to refuse his request. Then, something flashed behind her eyes that made his heart seem to stop in his chest, and the guilt he felt over leaving her and everyone else slammed into him as hard as it first had over a decade ago.

Finally, as if it hurt her to do so, she said, *"How much?"*

"How much what?"

Mila rolled her eyes, something Samson remembered her doing with annoying frequency when they were younger, an odd Two Leg quality for a feline. *"How much do you love her?"*

Samson's response was immediate, and though he knew it would hurt her, he also knew it was the right one.

"Like the moon loves the night and the sun loves the day."

He was right, it did hurt her. He watched with an ache in his heart as the pain flashed behind her eyes. This was something only mates said about one another, something that, once upon a time, in a different world where different things might have happened, Mila and Samson were supposed to say to each other.

Her voice was a pitch lower in his head when she spoke, just hardly above a whisper. *"You'll have to prove it."*

"I know."

Mila studied him, and Samson was very aware of the way her silver eyes ran over his body. *"Are you up for it?"* she asked.

Samson tilted his head, giving her a look that said that was a stupid question. Mila rolled her eyes again. Some things just never changed.

"I suppose you'll have to be," she continued. *"I can't imagine what sort of test my father will give for you to gain his assistance. He won't be pleased with all of this."*

"I know."

Mila huffed again and circled around Samson. He followed, thinking that maybe he wasn't up for this after all. He knew what the reaction would be to his arrival, knew his choices would be seen as traitorous, knew this would probably be one of the most difficult things he'd ever had to do, aside from leaving them all in the first place.

But what choice did he have? He'd meant what he said.

He really did love Surah like the moon loves the night and the sun loves the day. Even if it was such a hopeless, reasonless love.

Often times, the greatest of such is just so.

2 3

BLACK HEART

*H*e loved the reaction she gave every time she saw him.

She looked over from the tree branch on which she was perched, her head cocking in that bird-like way. Her wide, slanted eyes glittering, the shimmering wings on her back fluttering. Bits of pink leaves floated down to the earth as she bounced up and down, shaking the branch, the claws on her feet digging into the bark.

"Michael!" she trilled. Her head cocked from side to side. "Michael is here! Wonderful! Michael is here, everyone!"

Black Heart came forward, ignoring the looks from the Fae Queen's guards as he stepped into her palace, which was ringed with a high stone wall and composed of all earth and trees. The weather was always pleasant here, warm and moist, the sun filtering down gently through the multi-colored trees and creating rainbows where there should be shadows.

Black Heart loved this place.

"My love," he said, coming to a stop beneath the tree in which she was perched, his neck tilted back to look at her.

She floated down from the tree gracefully, her long gown

143

flowing and shifting in color from purple to blue to pink. Her wings fluttered once, and she landed lithely on her feet, clapping her hands and grinning widely to reveal sharp teeth.

"My love! My love!" she sang. "My love has returned!"

She flicked her hands, shooing away the two Fae guards nearest them, and snatched up Black Heart's hand in hers the way a love struck child might do. She led him into her bedroom, which was just a close ring of trees that were so thick they served as walls. The sun shined down overhead. A bed with a silk canopy sat in the center. This is where she led him.

"What's new?" she asked. "Tell me everything! It must be so exciting!"

Black Heart smiled, sat down on the bed. She immediately climbed on top of him. Her strange, beautiful face inches from his. His heart quickened.

"It is, my lady," he said, running his hands down her waist. "It is, indeed. It's going even better than I expected."

Her wide, slanted eyes sparkled. She clapped her hands, bouncing him up and down on the bed. "You've killed the Sorcerer King!" she giggled. "The king is dead! The king is dead!"

Black Heart grabbed her wrists and moved her arms around his neck, leaning up to kiss her soft throat. She giggled again softly.

"Not yet, my love," he whispered. "But soon. Very soon. I have his daughter, too."

She pulled back, the grin still wide on her face. "Surah Stormsong? You've captured her? Where is she? I want to meet her! Bring her to me! Bring her!"

Black Heart kissed her neck again. She shifted her hips, quieted.

"I have no intention of doing that," he said. "I'm going to kill her."

She pulled back, her red mouth drawing down into a pout.

She crossed her arms over her chest. "You have all the fun! Bring her here and *I* will kill her! A test! I'll give her a test she can't pass! It will be wonderful!"

Black Heart sighed and laid back on the bed, propping his hands behind his head. "Too dangerous, my love. I'm sorry, but no."

She bounced up and down again in anger, her legs tightening almost painfully around him. "I can make sure it gets done! You don't think I can! Shame on you, Michael! Shame on you!"

He stared up at her. "You didn't do so well with the Sun Warrior. You told me she would be hopelessly outmatched. What happened with that?"

The Queen's eyes narrowed and her voice lowered, as it only did when she was truly mad. She spoke between sharp, clenched teeth.

"She was," she said. "She *was* outmatched. I placed thirty of my best warriors against that girl, and she slaughtered them all like they were nothing more than annoying insects. You should have seen it! I underestimated Alexa. I won't make that mistake again. I will kill the Sorceress princess myself! You're selfish! That's what it is! You are a selfish man! Just like all men!"

He pulled her down to him roughly, pressing their bodies together, kissing her neck. She tried not to, but she giggled. He spoke softly against her skin. "Because of that, the Vampire King is dead, and I have only rumors to base the claim that he killed Syris Stormsong. I'm sorry, love. I won't risk it."

She pulled back again, a slight flush on her cheeks, her chest heaving. "Where is she now? The princess? Who is watching her?"

Black Heart hesitated. She threw up her hands, crossed her arms over her chest. "You left him with that brother of yours! Fool! You are a fool! He has proven he can't be trusted! Michael is a fool!"

His teeth clenched. "Watch your tongue, my love."

Her head cocked, grin slowly returning. "Or what? You'll cut it out?" She leaned down. "You just *try*! Just try! Just try!"

Black Heart smiled. She was so lovely when she was angry. "Of course not, my love. Wouldn't dream of it."

Her eyes narrowed. He pulled her to him again, their chests flush against one another's.

"He is my little brother, and he deserves one more chance to prove himself. I'm giving him that. Charlie loves me. I know he does."

She licked his throat, making him shiver. "But he also loves this princess," she mumbled against his skin. "You said he's loved her since he was a boy. Would *you* betray *me* for your Charlie Boy? Would you?"

Black Heart didn't know the answer to that question, but he knew what she wanted to hear.

"Of course not, my love."

"Fool! You are a fool then! Why not just kill the princess right now? You already have the Black Stone."

"There is no risk, so I am no fool. Even if Charlie does try to help the princess, I won't give him time to break her restraints. I'm going back as soon as I leave here. And as long as her father still has the White Stone, we need her alive for leverage. Each Stone is capable of canceling the power of the other, so I need them both before I make my move."

He lifted her skirt and ran his hands up her thighs, knowing this would cut off any response. Her skin quivered under his fingers. He kissed her neck. "Besides, I thought you'd be pleased I made time to see you."

She sat up and began working at his belt. "Of course!" she sang. "Always happy to see Michael! We will be quick! Princesses to kill and kingdoms to steal!" She laughed. "Quick! Quick! Quick!"

Black Heart smiled. "Quick enough."

THEO

She was lucky she was a woman.

He smiled and looked into her eyes. Of course, her cheeks brightened softly and she returned the gesture.

"I don't think you understand, Tyra," Theo said, voice as smooth as velvet. "Dark magic was used to portal into the castle by an...unsavory person. You were the person on watch over the security spells that are *supposed* to keep out just such people during the time of the breech." He tilted his head, regarding her with false gentleness. "Just explain to me how that can be. It is a matter of great importance."

Tyra's brow furrowed in thought, her cheeks still flushed from Theo's penetrating stare. He could tell just by her face that she was attracted to him, and he had no patience for idle talk just now. He could also tell she was hiding something.

He took a half step forward, leaning down to catch her eyes when they dropped to the floor. He placed his large hands gently on her shoulders. She looked up at him with wide eyes.

"It's all right, my lady," he said, his voice a low purr. "You can tell me what's on your mind."

Tyra looked down again. Then, all of a sudden, she burst

into tears, her chocolate hair falling into her face and her hands coming up to cover it. Theo raised an eyebrow and suppressed a sigh. This was exactly why women shouldn't be able to run kingdoms. They were always crying for no apparent reason. No control over their emotions.

Well, Surah had control. It was one of the reasons he liked her. He suppressed an eye roll and patted Tyra's shoulders.

"Tell me what troubles you," he said, his voice slightly less gentle.

She ran her sleeve underneath her nose, swiping at tears and snot. Theo swallowed back disgust and made sure his smile was in place.

Her voice trembled when she spoke. "I didn't have a choice, my Lord," she said.

More sobs racked her chest. Theo's eyes narrowed. "A choice in what?"

Her words came out so broken he could hardly understand her. "B-Black Heart…he…he had my *son!*" She was becoming hysterical. Theo let her continue. "He-he said he'd kill Tony if I didn't cooperate. I was so scared! You have to believe me!"

Theo's mouth was tight. "What did he ask you to do?"

She swiped at her nose again. "To lower the spells blocking portals inside the dungeons. I-I didn't know what to do. He had Tony! He had my son! He showed him to me through a vision spell, showed him bound and gagged and unconscious!" She grabbed his wrists. Theo resisted the urge to yank free of her touch. "What else could I have done?" she sobbed.

"Did he return your son?"

She nodded, her eyes hopeful. Theo turned to leave. "Then enjoy your time with him, because I'm sure that King Syrian will want you brought forth on treason."

Tyra began to sob again, asking over and over what else she could have done. Theo opened the door of her chamber and turned back, his gray eyes cold and hard.

"You could have been loyal to your kingdom," he said, and then he left. He could hear her sobs all the way down the hall.

He was angry. He basically had nothing to go on and time was running short. He could practically feel the heat of the situation on his neck. Everything he'd wanted for so long was just within reach. King Syrian had promised his daughter's hand, and all Theo had to do was find her. It was proving to be easier said than done.

But he was not quite out of ideas yet. There were others who might know more about the princess and her whereabouts.

The tiger was gone, having disappeared along with Surah, so he was out. Not that Theo would have relished trying to strike up a talk with that beast. That left the Warlock and Surah's two personal guards, Lyonell and Noelani.

He decided Bassil would be his next stop, and the Warlock had better be forthcoming. Theodine Gray's patience was wearing terribly thin.

25

SAMSON

Samson followed Mila through the jungle. She didn't say a word.

He wished he could explain himself to her in a way that wouldn't hurt her feelings, in a way she could understand, but he knew there was no use even trying. The ways of the jungle were too reinforced in her—too reinforced in all of them—that loving a Sorceress would sound like insanity.

Samson supposed it sort of was, but his instincts pushed him onward. He had a gut feeling that if he didn't reach Surah in time, it would mean her death. And, that, as insane as it may be, could not be allowed to happen.

He knew he would have to face his kind at one point or another, now was as good a time as any.

The two of them slinked through the undergrowth, the ground soft and moist beneath his paws. He kept tilting his head up to test the air, taking in the clean, untouched smell of it.

There were many things he missed about his home, and the smell was one of them. You didn't get air like this where there were people. You didn't get plants this green or silence this deep or sunlight as soft as this, either.

Mila kept moving onward, no doubt leading him to her father. She didn't look back even once to see if he was still following, didn't slow down to make sure he wouldn't lose her. She navigated her way over downed trees and swam across cool rivers and slipped between the plants easily.

Samson, though he was nervous about the task ahead, liked watching her move. She was so at home here, her powerful muscles shifting under her dark fur, silver eyes flicking back and forth. Her head and tail were held low, her progression silent. Mila had grown into a fine female while he'd been away. An alpha.

This made him think of Surah, as most of his thoughts led him to. People didn't label themselves alphas, but if they did, the princess would certainly be one of them. He wondered what she was doing just now, knew she was probably scared but calm, trying to figure her way out of whatever situation she'd found herself in. He supposed that made two of them.

Mila came to a stop in front of him, and Samson was so absorbed in his thoughts that he had to lock his forelegs so as not to run into her. Her head swiveled as she looked back at him.

"You sure you want to do this?" She asked him silently.

Samson's tongue flicked out, running over the blue and black fur around his mouth. *"Yes,"* he said.

She stared at him a moment, her round, silver eyes pinned to his. She looked like she didn't want to say what she said next. *"You'll probably be fighting Reno."*

Samson looked at her a moment, then laughed internally. *"Reno? You think I should be worried about fighting Reno?"*

She didn't seem to share in his amusement. *"He's not the same as he was when you left. He's no longer a cub. He's grown strong. Fighting him is no laughing matter."*

Samson went to move around her. *"I'm sure he has. Don't worry. I'll be fine."*

Mila blocked his path, her head held low between her muscular shoulders.

"I'm not worried," she snapped. *"What have I to worry about? I accepted your death a long time ago. It's you who should be worried. Reno has lived life here, among the beasts, while you have laid atop fluffy pillows on the bedroom floor of a Sorcerer princess. You would be a fool to underestimate him."*

Samson raised his head, the fur on his back standing on end. He decided it would be best not to respond to that. It might just come out in a growl.

She whipped her head back around and began to move forward again. *"Fine. Have it your way."*

Mila led him into darker, thicker vegetation, and at a few points, Samson had to crouch low to pass under thick tree branches that scratched at his back in a sort of pleasant way. The sunlight was muted to a dim glow in these places, where the green above was so thick and heavy it seemed as though you could walk on it.

Samson's heart kicked up in pace with each step he took. But Mila didn't know what she was talking about. Reno may have grown up in the jungle, but just in the past week Samson had battled demons and a Great Eagle for his Sorceress.

Living with Surah, protecting her and loving her, were not easy things. Over the years he had faced things more terrifying than even the jungles could offer. And his mind was sharp. Dealing for so long with people had made it so. Beasts were fearsome creatures, with sharp fangs and claws and deadly strength; what you saw was what you got. But people plotted and deceived and cheated and covered it all with smiling masks. People were far more dangerous. The true Kings of the Jungle.

Samson could handle this.

He hoped.

At last, the vegetation thinned, and Samson stepped into a large clearing where the sunlight managed to reach the earth.

The ground was a deep, healthy green, spotted with the most vibrant red and purple flowers in all the lands. Straight ahead, relaxing in the daylight, was a pride of twenty large felines, whose heads perked up as Samson stepped forward.

Above them all, staring down from a large rock near the stream running through the center of the open place, sat Drake, Mila's father. The cat who called himself king of this land. The one who had offered his daughter's hand in marriage to Samson's father so long ago.

Samson lifted his head, amber eyes watching both the king and his followers, thinking he would be lucky if he got through this with only having to face Reno in battle. If Drake had his lot attack, Samson wouldn't make it out of here alive.

Mila led him forward, silver eyes also watching her father, who was now standing atop the rock, his ears perked forward, nose testing the air, sampling the scent of the newcomer.

The sunlight caught in his dark fur and revealed hints of midnight blue amongst the black. His eyes were round and silver, like his daughter's, and by the time Mila came to a stop only fifteen feet from the rock on which her father stood, Samson could tell that Drake knew exactly who he was.

He hadn't heard the voice in all these years, but as soon as Samson heard the king speak in his head, the memories came flooding back to him. Drake's voice was a deep, rumbling, almost chocolaty sound. He said one word.

"Samson?"

Samson lowered his head respectfully. *"Yes, my king."*

Drake's eyes flipped to his daughter. *"What is this, Mila?"*

Mila's tail swished low, back and forth. Samson could tell she was nervous, despite her having said she didn't care what happened to him. But her voice sounded clear and strong when she spoke.

"He has come for our help, father," she said.

Drake looked back at Samson. *"Really? How is it that a dead cat can need help?"*

Samson said, *"As you can see, my king. I am not dead."*

Drake's eyes narrowed to slits. *"Then I am not your king. You have not been living among us."*

Samson raised his head, bringing himself to his full height. To show weakness here would be a death sentence. *"No, I have not. But I come willing to prove myself worthy of your assistance."*

"What is it you want?"

"I believe there may be a Sorceress held prisoner in your land. If I'm correct, I'm sure you know about it. I just want to know where she is."

The king was silent for a moment, silver eyes staring down at Samson, who held his gaze steadily. Then Drake laid back down atop his rock again, lowering his head between his paws. Samson held his breath.

"So be it," Drake said finally, his eyes flicking to the group of huge cats that were watching with keen interest to the left.

He called out Reno's name, just as Mila had predicted, and Samson had to admit he was impressed with how much his old friend had grown. He was no longer a scrawny cub, but had become a large alpha, matching Samson in weight and size. Reno moved toward the rock where they were standing, his wide chest out, dark head held high.

Samson met his stare. Reno's voice was edged with a growl when he spoke in his head. *"We thought you were dead."*

Samson sighed internally. *"I'm not."*

"Enough," Drake said. *"Move out into the clearing and get on with it before I get bored and decide to kill you both."*

Mila went to stand beside her father, flicking a nervous look between Samson and Reno, who were walking side-by-side toward the open place that served as the arena for just such a competition.

Reno's head tilted as he looked over at Samson. *"Where have you been?"* he asked.

Samson didn't want to answer, but he did anyway. He didn't see any point in lying now. *"Living with a Sorceress."*

"The one you're looking for?"

"Yes. Is she here?"

"You haven't earned that information yet...A Sorceress, huh? You always were a big dumb cat."

"And your talk was always bigger than your bite."

"Not anymore, my old friend."

"Let us see, shall we?"

"Certainly."

The two cats separated and moved to face each other, powerful muscles bunched and heads held low between their shoulders. Samson saw his own excitement reflected in Reno's black eyes. Without signal, Reno pounced, sharp claws extended, deadly teeth bared.

Samson leapt to the side, his paw lashing out and scraping Reno's side as he sailed by him. Reno growled, low and deep and rumbling, and it was answered with roars from the other cats on the sidelines, filling the quiet clearing with their calls.

Samson was already charging forward. He caught Reno in the side, the two of them crashing to the earth and rolling in a terrible display of teeth and claws. Blood and chunks of fur flew as fangs found purchase again and again.

Samson disentangled himself and charged again, his amber eyes narrowed and glittering. His ears were flat on his head, his heart racing and thumping in his chest, blood pumping hot and fast.

Reno's paw lashed out and caught him across the face, and Samson returned the blow with one of his own, shaking his head at the stars bursting behind his eyes.

Mila had been right. Reno had learned a thing or two in Samson's absence. He needed to end this, and quickly.

He stepped back, calculating his next attack the way people calculated theirs. It was a thing that had taken Samson years to master, being able to step out of his animal instincts in the heat of battle and use his mind. Surah had taught him to do it.

Reno was doing no such thing, he pounced forward again, and Samson crouched low and leapt upward, locking his powerful jaws around the underside of Reno's thick neck. Reno growled and snapped, trying to knock Samson free with all four paws as the two of them tumbled to the ground again.

Samson tightened his hold, locking his jaws just short of crushing capacity around the other cat's throat, his huge claws digging into his thick fur for even more purchase.

He held Reno trapped beneath him. Reno went still. Samson had him in a death hold and they both knew it.

When Reno chuffed in surrender, Samson released him slowly, back-pedaling and not taking his eyes off his opponent. His head was still low, his mouth bloody and his body scratched and battered and bleeding in various places. Reno looked even worse off, but he found his feet, his head and tail lowered in defeat.

Samson watched him closely, knowing that some beasts had a way of not accepting loss. But after a moment of hard staring Reno turned and limped his way back to the other cats, licking at his wounds.

Samson felt like doing the same, but this was not over yet, and there was simply no time for weakness.

He slowly approached the rock on which Drake was still perched, his chest pushed out and head high, tongue flicking out and tasting the blood still ringing his mouth. He bowed again to the king, his massive head coming down between his shoulders.

Drake's deep voice sounded in his head. *"Still as fearsome as ever, I see."*

Samson said nothing, only watched the king with wary eyes.

"I will make a deal with you, Samson, and if you agree, I will provide the information you have asked for."

Samson's heart sunk. He had been expecting something like this.

"What deal?" he asked. *"I want only to know where the Sorceress is, and then I will leave your land and I will not return."*

Mila shook her head once, but Samson didn't look at her.

Drake stood now and hopped down from his place on the rock, approaching Samson boldly. Drake was the biggest cat Samson had ever known, and the most people-minded of the bunch as well. Samson supposed he had to be to rule over the beasts of the Southlands jungle for so long, but it also meant that Samson was probably about to be faced with an unfavorable decision.

Drake held his head above Samson, looking down at him with sharp eyes. *"I will tell you where the Two-Leg Sorceress is if you agree to the arrangement that your father agreed to fifteen years ago."* His head swiveled as he looked back at where Reno was still nursing his wounds.

"You are stronger than my strongest, as you have just proven, and that makes you the only proper suitor for my daughter. The only cat fit to rule this land following my demise."

Samson's eyes flicked to Mila, who looked slightly horrified, which was comical on her feline face. But there was absolutely nothing comical about this situation.

Samson didn't like to do it, but there was another thing he had learned from living with people for so long, and that was how to lie.

"You have a deal, my king," he said.

Mila looked at him now, her silver eyes round and shimmering. He could tell just by the look there that she knew he was lying, that she was thinking of what he had told her to get her to bring him here.

"How much do you love her?" she'd asked.

"Like the moon loves the night and the sun loves the day."

Yes, Mila knew he was lying, and for a moment he feared she would share this information with her father, but she didn't. She just tore her gaze away. The hurt look behind her eyes made Samson's chest ache, but he was beyond grateful for her silence.

Drake didn't even consider the possibility that he was being fooled. Why would he? One did not lie to a King of Beasts.

"A couple of two-legs in all black led your Sorceress through the jungle early this morning," Drake said, accepting the matter as done. *"He had a dark power radiating from him, so the beasts let him be. He stashed her on the far edge of the land, where the sun rises in the morning, in a small space behind a wall of water. I have been told you can follow the trail once in the area, but have not been out to check myself. Two-legs yielding dark powers are dangerous creatures."*

"Thank you, my king." Samson said, and turned to leave, anxious to get to where he was going now that he had a location. He knew this land, and he would find his princess. He just hoped he wouldn't be too late. The eastern side of this jungle was at least an hour's travel from here. More running. He wondered if he would ever just get to nap today.

"I expect you to uphold your end of this deal, Samson," Drake, the King of Beasts, called after him.

Samson turned his head and looked back, but his eyes found Mila's and held them. He did not feel at all good about his next words. *"And so I shall, my king."*

Then, he left, racing eastward to save the person who his allegiance was truly to, feeling damned if he did and damned if he didn't.

Tired and hurting and worried and just damned.

26

SURAH

er hands hurt. They throbbed and pulsed and felt ten degrees warmer than the rest of her body, which was covered in sweat.

Her fingertips were blue and her mouth felt dry. The left side of her face hurt where the back of Black Heart's hand had struck her. She stared into the waterfall, listening to the sound of the rushing liquid and wondering how much time had passed.

Too much. That's how much.

Surah shoved the thought away, careful not to move her throbbing wrists. Her back was beginning to ache from the slumped position, and she rolled her neck slowly, trying to work out the muscles there. It wasn't really helping.

She was starting to really think about the possibility that she may not escape. She could perform simple magic without her piece of the White Stone, but none of it would be of use here.

She let out a long breath and looked up at the ceiling of the little cave. It wasn't so much the thought of dying that pained her—though it scared her, admittedly—but rather the people she loved and how she might not get to see them again.

It was the probability that if she died, her father would die too. It was that she may never get to run her fingers through Samson's thick fur again, or see his wide, amber eyes staring at her in that open way, a way he only had with her, and she only with him. It was Lyonell and Noelani, how she knew they would blame themselves for whatever happened. Even Theo would be sad, she knew.

No, it wasn't so much the thought of her own death that pained her. It was the way they would all grieve. She knew the feeling well, the empty, aching feeling it would bring them. She didn't want them to feel that. She didn't want to die.

A single tear sprang from her eye and rolled down her cheek, hot and wet. She'd been restraining them for the past twenty minutes or so. She wished so badly she could reach up and wipe it away, because she didn't want it to leave a trail there that would be visible to her captors. They could kill her, but they would not see her cry. They didn't deserve to.

Surah tilted her head to the side, trying to brush the tear off on her shoulder without raising it so the cuffs wouldn't tighten any further. It was a more difficult task than one might think. Her wrists shifted. She bit back a cry of pain. It came out in a sort of grunt.

"Got an itch?"

Her head snapped up at the voice, her heart jumping into her throat. The urge to wipe at her face to make sure it was clear of salt water struck her. She resisted. Barely. Her mouth fell open, and she tried to quiet her suddenly heaving chest.

"Yes, actually, Mr. Redmine," she said, finding her composure very quickly under the circumstances. She was proud of herself. "I've got an itch. I've had several of them in the past ninety minutes or so I've been chained here. Thanks for asking."

Charlie was silent for a moment, green eyes staring at her. "It just looked like you were trying to rub your face is all." He said, and paused. "And it's only been about seventy-five minutes."

Surah raised her chin, clenching her teeth so it wouldn't tremble. "It felt like seventy-five hours."

Charlie's mouth pulled up a bit in that smirk, making a dimple appear on his right cheek. "I missed you too, honey," he said.

Surah felt her anger come rushing back. "Did you see Bassil?" she snapped, ignoring his inappropriate address. "Did he know a way to break these restraints?"

Charlie nodded slowly. "Well… Yes, I guess."

"What the hell does that mean?"

"You're not going to like it, and you're already mad."

Surah looked indignant. "Ridiculous. I'm not mad. You haven't seen me mad."

His head tilted as he looked at her. "Sure I have, and you only curse when you get mad."

Her eyes narrowed. "You're wasting time, Mr. Redmine."

"I know."

She almost threw her hands up, but remembered just in time that she couldn't. Her teeth ground together instead.

"What is this?" she asked. "What have you to gain from tricking me this way? You already have me captive. Do you get some sick pleasure out of this, Mr. Redmine?"

Charlie sighed, running a hand over his short, dark beard. "Of course I don't," he said, as if that were the silliest accusation in the world. He pulled out a vial of silver liquid and held it up so she could see it.

Her lovely face lit up.

"Bassil gave that to you," she said. "I recognize the vial." Her violet eyes flicked up to his. "You really did go see him, then. He knew a spell that would break these." She smiled, pink lips turning up at the corners. "Of course he did. Bassil knows more spells than anyone I know."

"Yeah," he said, and paused. "Something like that."

Surah looked up at him, face wary again instantly. Charlie held up his hand before she could say anything.

"Let me explain," he said. "Yes, Bassil knew a spell he thought could work…but he didn't exactly explain very well *how* to get it to work."

Surah laughed shortly, her shoulders relaxing when she hadn't known they'd been tight. "I can perform the spell, Mr. Redmine. I have trained in all magics since I was a child. Just pour the potion over my wrists and tell me the words I need to know."

Charlie moved toward Surah and took a seat in front of her, folding his large body to the ground. He was close enough that she could hear his slow, steady breaths, could smell the clean scent of him. His handsome face was as unreadable as ever, but Surah thought it was more carefully so than usual. She tried not to let the green of his eyes capture her as he faced her, but it seemed somehow inevitable when he was so near.

She fumbled for words, surprised anew every time he made her do so. "I don't understand," she said. "There must be words to the spell. Tell me what Bassil told you, word for word, if you can."

"The Warlock said, 'Hate is what binds us. It is what traps us in place and refuses to let us move forward. It's the driving power of dark Magic and troubled minds and bad deeds.'"

Surah listened with growing horror. "And what sets us free?" she asked, though some part of her already knew the answer.

"Love," Charlie said in a near whisper. "Love sets us free."

Surah pulled her gaze away from him so she could think for a moment, staring down at her hurting hands. When she looked up again, there was hope in her violet eyes.

"Did you get a chance to ask him if he'd ever performed this spell before? What words he used if he did?"

Charlie nodded. "Yes and yes. He said he performed it once, and he used a nursery rhyme."

"A what?"

"A nursery rhyme. You know, like the ones that mothers—"

"I know what a nursery rhyme is."

"Okay."

A string of expletives ran through Surah's head. Her mind was trying to fly a mile a minute and instead was stuck at a stop. A spell that came with no definite language. She concentrated, running back over every bit of her training she could remember. She had learned something about such magic, she was sure of it. She just had to find the memory in a whole ocean of memories.

She looked at him again, this handsome, mysterious man who she still didn't know if she could trust. She seemed to be changing her mind about him around every corner.

Right now, he seemed like the only hope she had. Some of her memories came back at this thought, and a small smile found her face.

"So is that it then?" she asked. "That's what he told you was the driving force of the spell? If there is no definite language, then the words used must have a specific meaning, right?"

Charlie nodded slowly, rubbing his hand over his jaw. He looked the princess in the eyes, his glittering like jewels in the dark closeness of the cave.

"That's right," he told her. "The Warlock said the words must speak the language of love."

27

———

SURAH

Surah's eyebrows shot up.

Love.

Of course. Now she remembered. It all came back to her in a rush. Bassil had taught her this after the war in which she'd lost her mother and her sister. She had been in a bad place, angry at the world and filled with grief and hate. She remembered what he'd said to her now, word for word.

"No matter the horrors you see in the world, be careful not to allow yourself to be full of hate, princess. Hate is a heavy thing. It weighs us down, chaining us in a dark place... You focus instead on your love. If you want to be free of this heavy darkness you feel, focus on love. Love is the skeleton key to the chains which hate can wrap around you. To love is to be free."

She was pretty sure she'd rolled her eyes when he'd told her this. But she wasn't rolling her eyes now. She was thinking. Thinking very hard.

When Bassil had performed this spell he'd used a nursery rhyme, like the ones mothers sing to their children. What did she know of Bassil's mother? Not much, except that he'd lost her when he'd been very young. He rarely spoke of his mother,

164

or about anything in his past, actually, but Surah was sure there had been hints about it in all the years that she'd known the Warlock. He was her instructor, after all, and the best she'd ever had. To teach that well, one taught with heart and soul, with experience and learned lessons. Now she just had to prove a worthy student and put the pieces together.

And she needed to do it quickly.

Bassil loved his mother, she knew that, but Surah thought that he hadn't known his mother very well, because she had died when he'd been so young. She knew he probably wished he'd had a chance to know her, bet he wondered how his life would have been different had she lived on. This was all speculation of course, but it was based on an overall impression she had of the Warlock, and at least it was a start.

So he'd used a nursery rhyme to perform a spell that could break the chains of Dark magic. Could the nursery rhyme be one of the only memories Bassil had of his mother? She couldn't be sure, but she thought this was right. Her gut said it was right, because words that meant so much to someone could create powerful magic indeed.

Charlie was silent as she worked through all this, and now she wasn't sure who would be a better choice to perform the spell. She was trying hard to think of something her mother used to say to her, but other than simple *I love yous*, most of the things she remembered her mother telling her were about how to be a proper princess.

She thought of her sister, but it had been so long since she'd lost Syra that the memories were a distant thing, something she'd probably blocked out long ago so she could get on with her life, and now it pained her to think that she'd done so.

Her brother and father were not men who often spoke words of love, they more so showed their care through their actions. She couldn't think of a nursery rhyme, or a lullaby, or even a simple sentence that meant so much to her.

It was such a heavy, defeating thought.

"What're we going to do, princess?" Charlie asked.

Surah bit her lip, her eyebrows furrowed with worry. "I don't know, Mr. Redmine," she said. "I seem to be drawing a blank."

"You must know something, some memory that, I don't know, can fuel this thing."

She stared at him a moment, at the strong line of his jaw. She shook her head slowly. "If I do, it won't come to me right now. I have to think. I don't suppose you have anything that can do it?"

Charlie was silent for a long time, his emerald eyes going deep in thought.

"You do?" she asked, her heart leaping with hope.

His shoulders lifted once in a small shrug. "I have to think."

"We don't have much time."

"I know."

Surah sighed and swallowed, wishing she could run her arm across her damp forehead.

"All right," she said. "We may as well get started, because Gods know how long this is going to take. Pour the powder on my wrists and then place your hands on mine. We'll both just have to concentrate. Say whatever words come to you that you associate with love. I'll do the same." She glanced at the softening daylight beyond the waterfall. "Maybe we'll get lucky."

He did as she asked, popping the cork out of the vial and sprinkling the silver substance over her wrists, where it caught and hung in the black smoke that was holding her in place, like stars dusted over a dark sky.

His large, warm hand closed over her numb fingers, which had gone from pulsing heat to terribly cold. His touch soothed her some, even through her thick gloves, and she found herself catching her breath.

"Ready?" she asked.

"Sure."

She took a deep breath and closed her eyes. After a moment, he did the same.

They tried. And tried and tried. He said things that his mother used to say to him, and she did the same, but they had no effect.

Surah reached back in her mind and recalled the brunches she used to have with Syra and her mother, of the times they'd shared tea and secrets. She thought of Samson, of how he would always call her "love" or "honey" or "sweetheart" when they were alone, of how he would lick her wounds when she was injured.

But nothing worked. The chains remained as immovable as ever. She wouldn't have thought such a task would be so hard, but then she supposed that it really would be for most anyone. Who, when faced with this situation, with the clock practically ticking between their ears, could think of words that meant so much to them that they could set them free? It was a lot harder than one would think.

Twenty minutes passed. They were both sweating heavily now.

Thirty minutes. Surah was starting to get a headache behind her closed eyes. Charlie's hands were growing moist.

Forty minutes, and at last, Surah opened her eyes, releasing a heavy breath.

"It's useless," she said, and didn't even care that her voice sounded uncharacteristically small.

Charlie's eyes opened and he looked at her. She was looking down at her hands, her face blank of any expression at all. He reached a hand up and placed it under her chin, gently tilting her face up to look at him. She offered no protest.

"No," he said. "It's not. We have to keep trying. It'll work. It has to."

She shook her head, fighting back more tears. "No, it doesn't."

"Yes, it does."

She cleared her throat. "Why?"

"It just does."

Surah looked down at her hands again, to afraid to believe him. Charlie sighed and looked around, his eyes falling on his old wooden guitar, where it rested against the wall. Black Heart had left it there as a joke, commenting that it was so that Charlie didn't get bored on prisoner duty.

He got up to retrieve the instrument and settled back down in front of her, the guitar across his lap.

She watched him as his fingers settled over the strings, his hands moving the guitar into position. "You have an idea?" she asked.

He nodded, swallowed. "Yep."

"A song?" she asked, and smiled, hope flooding back into her. "You know a song that speaks about love? What song is it?"

"You've never heard it before."

"I know a lot of songs."

"Not this one."

"How do you know?"

He hesitated, and when his eyes met hers, she saw something there that she couldn't quite pin down.

"Because," he said, "I wrote it and I've never played it for anyone before."

Her smile grew. This might actually work. "What's it called?"

Again, he hesitated. "It doesn't have a name," he said.

For some reason, Surah thought this was a lie.

Surah waited silently. Charlie pulled his eyes away, looking down at the instrument in his lap.

"Just play it," she said gently. "It's worth a shot."

Charlie nodded, still staring at the strings. He took a deep breath and began to play. His fingers began to strum the strings slowly, releasing a gentle melody. Then they moved a little faster, not much, but a little, the chords taking on a soft rhythm that made goose bumps pop up along her arms. Before he even began to sing the words, Surah could tell this was a love song. Just the soft, sweet notes said it was.

Then Charlie began to sing, his deep voice a perfect pitch that accompanied the melody. More goose bumps worked their way across her neck, and she found herself watching his lips move as he sang the words. She listened. She had a feeling that when Charlie Redmine picked up his guitar and played a song, anyone within hearing distance stopped and listened. But it was just the two of them in the small, slowly darkening cave. Just them and the music and his deep, country voice. A humble, beautiful drawl.

The words were simple, lovely.

"In a world full of darkness
And a dream where it's cold
Amongst the shadowed stardust
There's a princess I'm told
She is not like the others
She is good and she is sweet
Where there is fault she offers mercy
Where others bind, she sets free..."

The world seemed to have fallen away. Surah could no longer feel the pain in her wrists, the ache in her back. She could no longer hear the clock ticking between her ears. All she could hear was Charlie. His deep voice and sweet song and the beating of her heart. He continued to play, filling up the cave with the soft music, filling up the world with it.

"In a world full of darkness
And a dream where it's cold
Amongst the shadowed stardust
There's a princess I'm told"

The tempo picked up again here, his fingers strumming the strings with rapid movements, dancing over them. Surah felt her own pulse quicken, her throat go tight, a knot forming in the pit of her stomach.

The music slowed again, coming to an end, and Charlie's voice was so quiet as he sang the final words that she had to strain to hear. She didn't realize it, but she was leaning forward.

"Sleep well, princess
Rest your lovely head
Wherever you are in the world
I wish I was instead"

Surah's hammering heart stopped. Her breath halted in her throat. Charlie's fingers stroked the strings slowly, then settled. The last chord hung in the air for a bit, as if she could reach out her hand and touch it, and then silence fell around them.

She stared at Charlie and was surprised to find that he was not looking up at her. His eyes were downcast, an opposite to his usual direct stare, and she wondered if his cheeks were slightly red under his dark facial hair. There was no way to know.

No way to know, but she did, didn't she? She could feel it. She could hear it whispered on the notes that had faded away and yet seemed to still be lingering in her ears. She could see it on his face, in the emerald of his eyes that would no longer meet her own.

Perhaps it was presumptuous of her, perhaps she was completely off the mark, but she didn't think so. She thought the song just might belong to her, despite the fact that she had no real reason to believe this. Just a feeling.

She wanted to ask him, but found she didn't have the nerve. How arrogant would that sound? She couldn't just say, hey, you wrote that for me, didn't you? No, she couldn't say that. She wouldn't say that. She opened her mouth to say it.

For whatever reason, she had to know.

But she didn't get the chance, because in front of her, Charlie's eyes widened, and she followed his gaze to see what had made them do so. While listening to his song she had completely forgotten about the restraints around her wrists. She had forgotten about everything, the whole situation, and now that the music had stopped, it all came back with crushing clarity.

She couldn't believe what she was seeing.

The black smoke holding her in place was loosening. The relief was instant, though pain still coursed through her fingers. She watched as the black magic receded and folded into itself, then disappeared altogether.

She wiggled her fingers. It took more effort than it should have. There were angry, red rings around her wrists, like bloody bracelets. She could feel the blood slowly beginning to course back through her fingers, and it felt wonderful and awful at the same time.

She was free.

Without thinking, she threw her arms around Charlie's neck and pulled him into a tight hug, breathing in the fresh scent of him, absorbing his heat.

Slowly, his strong arms came up and held her even tighter, their bodies pressed close together, his chest warm and solid against hers.

"Thank you," she whispered against his neck, thinking she should pull away. Lingering.

He was silent for a moment. Then, he said, "You're welcome."

"Well, isn't this just precious?" said a voice beside them.

Charlie and Surah broke apart instantly, hearts leaping in their chests, eyes going wide like children who had just been caught doing something naughty.

They saw him at the same time, saw the Black Stone weighing heavily around his neck and the murderous glint in his emerald eyes.

Black Heart had returned.

The heels of his boots clicked as he stepped forward, his

dark cloak rippling like something alive as he moved. His pale hands came up and slipped the hood back from his head, revealing his dark, slicked-back hair. He was smiling, but there was only malice behind it, making it an oddly terrifying expression. The antithesis of a smile.

Black Heart clucked his tongue, cold eyes flicking back and forth between Charlie and Surah, who were now on their feet, postures stiff. His eyes settled on Charlie and he shook his head.

"I'm disappointed in you, Charlie Boy," he said. "*Extremely* disappointed."

2 8

—————

SURAH

*S*ilence hung between them for what seemed to Surah to be an incredibly long moment. It was as though time itself had paused, as if everything in the universe hung suspended in space.

Waiting.

Then, Charlie said, "I guess that makes two of us, brother."

Surah's head jerked toward Charlie, her mind momentarily unable to process coherent thoughts. Charlie Redmine was staring levelly at his brother.

Black Heart shook his head again, his hand coming up and rubbing his jaw. Surah realized this must be a habit for both men, except it was somehow attractive when Charlie did it.

"What am I supposed to do with you now, Charlie Boy? You haven't left me many choices."

Charlie's voice answered smooth and calm. "There are plenty of choices."

Surah stood perfectly still, saying nothing. Black Heart looked at her, and she tilted her chin up and held his gaze. He laughed.

"Still so proud, are we?" he asked, taking a step toward her.

173

Surah held her ground, but to her surprise, Charlie moved between her and his brother. His voice sounded more serious than she'd ever heard it when he spoke.

"Leave her alone, Michael," he said.

The anger that flashed behind Black Heart's eyes was so intense that Surah thought she could feel it burning his skin, but she didn't step back. Charlie still stood in between them.

Black Heart's eyes fixed on Surah over Charlie's shoulder. His lips were tight when he spoke. "Move aside, little brother."

Charlie folded his arms over his chest. "No."

Black Heart's eyes flicked back to him. "Fine, have it your way."

His hand whipped to the side, and Charlie was lifted from his feet and slammed into the rock wall of the cavern, as if one of the Gods had reached down and slapped him aside. Black Heart's hand was raised, holding Charlie in place without even touching him.

Surah was already in motion.

She moved so fast that Black Heart's one moment of forgetting her was enough. She rushed forward, the sais that had been tucked under her cloak already clutched in her hands, which were still in pain from the restraints. She dropped to the ground and swept her leg around, knocking Black Heart hard in the legs and sending him down to his knees. Raising her weapons, she prepared to send them through his neck. She thrust them forward.

But Black Heart was no longer distracted, and before the sharp points of the sais could hit their mark, she was tossed into the air in the same way Charlie had been, scooped up and thrown aside by dark magic, her body becoming weightless.

She slammed into the stone wall hard on her left side, knocking her head against it and seeing stars. Pain shot down her body in a hot rush. Black Heart held her pinned to the wall, almost crushing her with the force of the Black Stone's power.

She couldn't move, could hardly breathe. This was it then, she was going to die. The thought made a silent terror boil inside her.

Black Heart was sweating, the Stone around his neck heavy and pulsing heat. The thing was fueled by hate and anger, and Black Heart had plenty of that to spare. But it still was not easy using so much power. He was getting better at it, and soon, he would be unstoppable.

He held them both to the walls, like flies caught in a spider's web. His boots clicked as he approached Surah.

"I know what to do, little brother," he said, the smile returning to his face as he looked over his shoulder at Charlie.

Charlie's face was turning red, his eyes bulging in their sockets, but he managed to force words out between his teeth.

"Let her go, Michael."

Black Heart laughed, and Surah could do nothing but stare at the dark Sorcerer in terror.

"Oh, I think not, Charlie Boy," he said. His head tilted as his eyes fell back on Surah. "I think I will make you watch her die. Cure you of this…unhealthy obsession once and for all."

Charlie opened his mouth as if to yell, but Black Heart flicked his wrist, magic swirling around his fingers, and Charlie's snapped shut, cutting off his words.

Black Heart moved to stand in front of Surah. He smiled. "I'll give your regards to your father," he said. "Perhaps you two will meet in the heavens."

Surah shook her head. "No, we won't," she said.

Black Heart's head tilted again, his eyes dark and amused and murderous. "Why is that, princess?"

Surah met his stare, held it. "Because I'll be waiting for you in hell."

Black Heart laughed, deep and bellowing, his wide shoulders shaking. Then, his laughter cut off abruptly, as if by a switch, and his hand came up and clenched into a fist.

Surah felt a crushing weight drop on her throat, cutting off her air completely. Her eyes bugged out of her sockets, and her vision went dark for a second before returning in a blurry haze. Her muscles jerked, but remained plastered to the wall. Her brain began screaming for oxygen. Didn't find any.

Black Heart leaned in close, the look on his face pure joy.

"In death you will finally learn how to hold your tongue," he said, and tightened his fist further still.

Now the world outside Surah's eyes went dark and stayed dark, and she knew she was only moments from slipping away, no matter how hard she tried to cling to the surface.

It was almost a relief.

29

SAMSON

Samson came to a stop when he reached the water. He lowered his head and lapped at it with his dry tongue, watching all around him, scanning the ground, the trees. She was near, he could feel her, could smell her, and this was where the trail ended.

After taking some water he lifted his head and scanned the surroundings again, spotting a waterfall some twenty yards upstream.

Behind a wall of water, Drake had said. Samson's gut told him that she was there. He made his way back to the trees and began his cautious approach.

Now that he was here, he knew he would need to move silently, carefully. It was no wonder that the beasts had steered clear of this area. The dark energy in the air grew thicker as he approached the waterfall. He could almost taste the Sorcerer in the air, the one who had hurt and captured his beloved Surah, and his killer instinct was set ablaze by the scent.

But Black Heart had the Black Stone, so Samson would need to wait for the perfect moment to strike, and if the foul energy exuding from the hidden cavern behind the waterfall was any indication, that moment was near.

He held his body low to the ground, creeping closer and closer. He could hear voices from inside the cave, made indistinguishable by the sound of the rushing water. His ears swiveled and perked, trying to make out what was being said. He needed to get closer.

He reached the waterfall and hopped onto the rocks at its edge, his paws landing silently and lithely. He listened again before moving forward, but the voices had stopped. They were no longer talking. Samson moved forward, the waterfall concealing him, and poked his head into the dimly lit space. What he saw made a red hot fury burn through his chest.

Surah hung on the wall like some macabre portrait, her limbs limp and eyes closed, pretty face a disturbing blue color.

Charlie hung on the opposite wall, his face twisted with silent agony as his eyes stared widely at Surah.

Black Heart stood in front of the princess, his back to Samson, his attention focused on killing her and making his brother watch. Samson decided right then that he did not want to kill this man, he *had* to. If it was the last thing he ever did, he had to.

He leapt forward into the air, his ascent soundless, his huge claws extended and large teeth bared. Black Heart's head turned just in time to see the tiger's terrifying face flying at him before Samson landed on his back and sent him crashing to the ground.

Black Heart tried to move his throat away, but Samson snagged the necklace holding the Black Stone around his neck between his teeth and snapped the chain, ripping it free. His head whipped to the side and the necklace flew over to the wall, the Black Stone making a sound like rock crashing into rock when it hit the wall. Then it clunked to the ground.

Charlie and Surah fell to the ground in the same moment.

Black Heart still had Surah's piece of White Stone, and he used it to portal out from underneath the tiger. He removed the sword from beneath his cloak, aiming it at Samson, who was standing over the Black Stone, his head low, amber eyes glowing, teeth bared.

Black Heart moved cautiously forward, his hair standing out around his head, his emerald eyes angrier than ever. He held his sword up and spoke between clenched teeth.

"I will kill you for that, you stupid beast."

Samson growled, the sound rebounding off the close walls of the cave like thunder. Black Heart portaled to the spot above Samson's back, planning to send his blade through the neck of the tiger. But Samson anticipated this move, and he leapt to the side, swiping at the Black Stone and sending it skidding over near Charlie, who was just finding his feet.

And Surah was finding hers.

She looked exhausted. There were blood-red rings around her wrists and more angry red marks on her neck. Her lavender hair was a mess atop her head, and her teeth were gritted in concentration.

She rushed forward with her sais. Black Heart turned just in time to block her strike with his sword, the weapons clinking together with the sound of metal on metal.

Samson sprang forward, and Black Heart spun around, slicing the air with his blade and sending the tiger skidding back out of the way.

Surah struck again. Black Heart evaded. He was faster than Sam would have thought, which was not a good thing. Samson kept trying to get at him, but Black Heart portaled out of the way again and again, doing a disappearing and reappearing dance all around them.

Meanwhile, Charlie Redmine was bending down to pick up the Black Stone. He took a deep breath as his fingers wound around it. He held it tight and said one word.

"Stop."

All three of them, Samson, Surah and Black Heart halted in their movements, their bodies freezing in place. Charlie's green eyes glowed as the dark power ran through him. It was no wonder his brother had gone insane. The power of the Black Stone was potent, noxious.

"Let me go, Charlie Boy," Black Heart said, watching his brother the way a lion will watch a pack of hyenas.

"Don't, Charlie," Surah said.

Samson just stared.

Charlie kept his fingers firmly locked around the Black Stone. He went over to where his brother was frozen in place and put a hand on his shoulder, looking into his eyes.

"I'm sorry, Mikey," he said.

Then, he moved over to Surah and Samson, taking her by the hand and placing his other on Samson's large back.

Black Heart's voice was an angry growl. "Charlie Boy... If you do this, you're better off just killing me now."

Charlie stared at Michael, and Samson knew that his words were no bluff. If Charlie did this, the line would be drawn, the decision irreversible. If he didn't, that same line would still be crossed, only he would be on the other side. He was stuck firmly between a rock and a hard place.

Surah's eyes flicked to Charlie, her hand in his, her fate heavy on his shoulders. Sam wasn't sure when it had happened, perhaps it was a combination of things, but he could see that she trusted Charlie Redmine, though she wouldn't admit it, not even to herself.

And though his face was that smooth, unreadable mask that seemed to be his default expression, Sam could tell by the look in Charlie's emerald eyes that this decision was not easy for him, that his heart was split clean down the middle, and he was faced with choosing which side to try and salvage.

Sam honestly did not know what his answer would be,

though looking back he supposed it should have been clear. They all stood in silence, the only sound that of the rushing water and the thumping of their hearts, and Charlie made up his mind.

For better or worse, and everything that would follow, he made up his mind.

He looked at his brother with too many emotions passing over his handsome face.

"I can't," Charlie said. "I can't kill you, Mikey. But I can't let you kill her, either."

And then he closed his eyes and portaled himself and the princess and her tiger out of there, the black magic from the stone engulfing them and tossing them across space and time.

The last thing they heard before leaving the jungle was Black Heart's howl of anger.

It sounded oddly like a nail being pounded into a coffin.

3 0

———

SURAH

They landed in Surah's bedroom in her father's castle, stumbling over their feet and falling to the ground in a heap. Charlie was not so great at portaling yet, and controlling the magic using the Black Stone was quite a task.

They laid sprawled out on the ground for several moments, trying to catch their breaths and slow their racing hearts. All of them were either injured or exhausted or both. Samson had travelled much further today than his body was built for, and his stomach heaved as he lay on his side panting, his long tongue lolling out of his mouth.

Surah was hurting all over. It would be easier to count the places on her body that were not in pain rather than the other way around. Her wrists were bleeding, her face was swollen, her head pounded, and the left side of her body was screaming sorely.

Charlie looked as though he was very close to heaving up the meager contents of his stomach, so nauseated he was from the trip. He couldn't seemed to catch his breath.

So they all just laid there. Surah climbed to her feet first, moving over to Charlie. Her lavender hair was a wavy mess around her face, which was pinched with worry.

"Are you okay?" she asked.

Charlie waved a hand, not even trying to make a move to stand. "I'll be fine," he said. "I should ask you the same."

Surah shrugged. "I'll live."

Charlie gave that charming smirk of his, still staring up at the ornate ceiling. "That's good."

"Well, I'm fine, too, love. Thanks for asking," Samson said in her head.

She moved over to him and ran her hands through his thick fur. Samson closed his amber eyes and chuffed a little at her touch.

"Thank you, Sam," she told him silently. *"You saved my life."*

Samson gave her a toothy smile, his eyes still closed. *"What else is new?"*

All of a sudden she remembered her father, who was dying from demon poison as they sat here taking stock of each other's injuries. She prayed to the Gods that it was not too late, that the poison could still be reversed.

She glanced at the grandfather clock that stood in the corner of the large room, a family heirloom that had been passed down to her from her mother. The hour read six-thirty, and Surah looked over at the arched windows to see the sunlight had nearly bled completely out of the sky.

Charlie had an arm draped over his face, but he lifted it and looked at her. As if he had read her thoughts, he held the Black Stone out for her.

"Here," he said. "Take it. Go save your father."

She didn't hesitate. She stepped forward and wrapped her fingers around the cold Stone, her hand brushing against Charlie's warm skin.

"Thank you," she said. "I am in your debt, Mr. Redmine."

Charlie draped his arm back over his face and waved his

hand again. "Don't worry about it, princess," he said. "Just go save the king."

Surah nodded. "What are you going to do?"

Charlie peeked out at her beneath his arm. "Lie here for a second, if that's all right."

"I second that," Samson said.

"Okay," she said, "but be quiet. If anyone finds you here…it won't be good."

Both Samson and Charlie gave small grunts.

Surah turned toward the door, moving quickly, but when she got there, she turned back. "And Charlie?"

Charlie lifted his head, his eyebrows raised over deep emerald eyes. Surah smiled at him. Not her princess smile, but her real one, and it felt right being there. Charlie returned it.

"Yes, princess?"

Surah opened the door, peering out into the long hallway to find it empty. Thank the Gods. She looked back at him once more.

"Call me Surah," she said.

Then she shut the door to the room and raced down the hall in the direction of her father's chambers, hoping beyond hope that she wasn't too late.

She was in such a hurry that she did not see Theodine Gray as she rushed by the doorway he was standing in.

SURAH

"Why isn't it working?"

Bassil lifted his hand and placed his palm on her father's forehead. "It *is* working, princess," he said. "His fever is already breaking. You just have to be patient. The demon poison has been in his system for too long. It could take several weeks for him to fully recover."

Surah's mouth fell open, and she snapped it shut and clenched her teeth, fighting back tears. It was hard to look at her father this way. She had never seen him look so bad before. His skin was a startling ashy white, like old chalk, and his usually perfectly combed hair sat in thin tangles atop his head. She could see his chest rising and falling with thin, rasping breaths, his eyes closed as if they would remain that way forever. He looked like a dying man.

All the emotions she had been bottling came rushing over her in a harsh wave, and her knees buckled. Bassil grabbed her elbows gently, supporting some of her weight, his face drawn with concern.

"Perhaps you should be resting, princess," he said. "You don't look well."

Surah shook her head and locked her knees, smoothing her cloak out with shaking hands. "I'll be fine," she said.

Bassil gave her a dubious look but offered no protest.

Surah moved a chair over by her father's bed and took a seat, staring at the Black Stone sitting atop her father's chest. She could see the black magic at work inside the stone, which seemed to slither and writhe, sucking out the poison that was running rampant in her father's body.

"I just want to stay with him for a while," she said. "I will rest as soon as I am able."

Bassil quirked an eyebrow. "You mean when you can no longer stand on your own two feet?"

Surah gave no answer, just sat watching her father, wishing he would open his eyes and smile at her. She knew Bassil was right. She was in more pain than she cared to admit at the moment, and the thought of crawling under her covers and falling into a deep sleep sounded like pure heaven.

But she would do no such thing. She would sleep in this chair if she had to. She wanted to be there when her father woke up. She had to, because despite what Bassil said, some panicked part of her feared that Syrian might not wake up at all. After all the events of the past two days, the thought of leaving him was just beyond her.

Bassil released a slow sigh. Then he bent at the waist and placed a small kiss on her forehead.

"All right, princess," he said. "Do as you please. I will be back in soon to check on you. I'll bring you some soup. I bet you don't even remember the last time you ate." His nose wrinkled. "And you may want to consider taking a bath. You don't smell good."

Surah smirked, but there was no humor in it. "Anything else, Warlock? I suppose you also want to tell me that I'm having a bad hair day?"

Bassil smiled. "As a matter of fact…"

Surah rolled her eyes. "Oh, just be gone with you," she said.

Bassil chuckled as he stepped out into the hall and shut the door behind him. He turned around to find himself face to face with Theodine Gray. The Head Hunter gave him an annoyed look. "Get out of my way, Warlock," he said.

"The king is resting, Hunter Gray."

Theo nudged Bassil aside. "I have no intention of waking him," he said, opening the door to the king's bedroom and shutting it in Bassil's face before the Warlock could protest.

Surah's head turned as he entered. She said nothing, just sighed internally and turned back to her father.

Theo took a few steps toward her. "I'm glad to see you've returned safely, princess," he said, and his eyes fell on the Black Stone resting on Syrian's chest. "And you've brought back the Black Stone as well. Impressive."

Surah's rubbed at her forehead. "Thank you, Hunter Gray," she said.

Theo spied the red ring around her wrist that peeked out of her cloak sleeve, and he stepped around the bed, anger spiraling in his eyes as he took in the black and purple bruise on the left side of her face.

"Who did that to you?" he asked.

Surah's voice sounded robotic when she spoke. She considered lying, but saw no point in it. "Black Heart," she said.

"So he did have you captive, then?"

Surah nodded, her eyes still glued to her father.

"And how did you escape?"

Surah looked up now. "If you don't mind, Hunter Gray," she said, using great effort not to speak between clenched teeth, "I would like some time to rest. I'm sure you will get all the details from my father, after I speak with him, but for now, I'm tired. It's been an extremely long day. I believe some silence is in order."

Theo gave a low bow, and Surah watched him closely as he

did so, unable to tell how he was taking this command. She didn't even really care if he was offended. She was too tired and hurt and worried to care.

Theo moved toward the door again, flicking his wrist so that it swung open. He stopped when he got there and looked back at her. She could feel his eyes on her, but she remained facing the bed.

"Of course, my princess," he said. "I've other things to attend to, anyhow."

Surah said nothing

In a light voice, he added, "I've got a prisoner to question and a very probable execution to arrange, pending trial, of course."

Surah's shoulders tightened a fraction. Her head turned to the side, looking at him over her shoulder, her violet eyes narrowed. "What are you talking about?"

"I don't want to scare you," he said. "But Charlie Redmine was found lying in wait in your chambers about an hour ago." He paused. Surah's teeth clenched at the dramatic effect. "Don't worry, princess. You're safe now. The traitor is locked away in the dungeons, and you have my word that it will be the last place he ever sees on this earth."

Theo shut the door behind him, leaving Surah alone with her unconscious father, her heart jackhammering in her chest.

She rubbed her forehead with her fingers and thought, *Well, shit.*

3 2

SURAH

wo days had passed and her father had yet to gain full consciousness. He awoke only a handful of times, and even then his eyes stayed just below half-mast, his voice coming out in nonsensical mumbles.

Surah was present for every awakening, leaning over his bedside and smiling down at him with unshed tears in her eyes. He was getting better. She could see that, but Bassil had been right about the king's recovery taking some time, which seemed to be the one thing she'd been running short on lately.

She stayed by her father as many hours of the day as she could spare, which was not as many as she would have liked. She had been a busy girl these past two days, tending to royal matters in her father's stead, making comforting speeches to the people, most of whom were completely unaware of how close they'd come to losing their king.

On top of that, she'd been trying to figure out how to clear Charlie Redmine's name. To put it truthfully, she'd been trying to find a way to save his life.

It wasn't as easy a task as one might think it should be.

The royals were angry, and understandably so, but that

189

didn't make their refusal to see reason any less aggravating. They were calling for blood in the names of their lost ones. She had spoken to several of them privately, including the parents of Merin Nightborn and Cynthian Lancer, to try and explain that Charlie Redmine was not like his brother, that he had assisted in her escape, that he had nothing to do with the murders of their children.

Lady Nightborn responded with a threat to take the matter to the public. Lord Lancer accused Surah of having a soft heart, of incapable of ruling because she was a female, and even used the word coward.

To say the least, the talks had gone less than well.

And to make matters worse, Theo seemed determined to keep his promise. Surah wasn't sure why Theo wanted Charlie dead, except that she suspected he knew more than he was letting on. She told herself that was silly, that there was no way Theo could know about the... relationship between her and Charlie, if you could even call it that.

She'd visited him in the dungeons, but only once, and for less than five minutes, just long enough to tell him she was trying to clear his name, to assure him she hadn't forgotten about him, and that everything would be all right.

But everything was not all right. Everything was about as far from all right as it could get.

Her father couldn't help her, not in his condition, and she knew the royals would not wait long enough for him to recover. Theodine Gray wouldn't wait, either. They wanted answers, an open and shut trial, and yes, an execution.

On top of that, Black Heart was still on the loose, probably plotting his crazy revenge.

The only fortunate thing so far was that Jude Flyer had been surprisingly eager to help when she'd come to him, asking him to defend Charlie. The pudgy little man's face had lit up, and he'd listened to Surah's story—with the understanding that it was completely confidential—with excited attentiveness.

She'd told him the truth, leaving out the parts that didn't seem to require adding, like the song Charlie had sung her to set her free, like the embrace they'd shared that had made her insides twist and her chest go warm. Those things had nothing at all to do with the matter.

Or so she kept telling herself.

But even with Jude Flyer's help, the odds of getting Charlie clear of the charges were not looking good, and Jude had told her this flat out. Charlie was the only witness to the murder of Merin Nightborn. The place she died was his establishment. He was the brother of a feared criminal, kin to a known outlaw. These things may all have been circumstantial, but all he had in his favor was the word of the princess, and grieving people could be relentless in their efforts for revenge.

They had a bird in the hand and they wanted its bones crushed under their fingers.

Surah sat in her chambers now, having sought a few moments of peace away from her father's room, which she had come to think of as the sick room. She sat up in the wide window sill beside Samson, her knees drawn up and tucked under her cloak.

She stared out at the kingdom below, at the ornate houses and tall towers, at the glittering lights and cobblestone pathways and red rooftops. People moved around down there, going about their lives as if nothing was wrong, completely unaware of the turmoil going on inside the castle.

This was why she envied them sometimes. It seemed like such a dream to be able to live life so simply, a thing she could only see but never touch.

She was not fit to rule a kingdom. She'd suspected so before, but she knew now. Her respect for her father had grown greatly. It was a terrible thing to be under this kind of pressure, to have people depending on her to do what was right and fix things, as if the things that were broken could even be fixed.

A knock sounded on her door, and she climbed down from the window and stood, smoothing out her cloak as she did so.

With a flick of her wrist, the door swung open, and Bassil stood there. The grave look on his face sent a shiver down her spine.

The Warlock entered the room and shut the door behind him, his patchwork cloak flipping with his rushed movements. Surah stepped forward, her pulse racing.

"What's going on?" she asked.

The big man said nothing, just took her by the hands and pulled her to a seat on the bed. Surah was surprised by this, but offered no protest. She was too busy just breathing.

"I'm afraid I have bad news, princess," Bassil said.

Surah's heart dropped. She'd suspected as much, but hearing him say it was worse. Her face was carefully void of expression, her voice painfully light.

"What news is that?"

Bassil's dark brown eyes held hers for a long moment. Then he said, "Charlie Redmine will not live to see the morning."

33

SURAH

Surah couldn't think of a single thing to say.

She just sat there, staring at him, her face smooth and blank. After several minutes, Bassil cleared his throat. "Those who are angry have arranged his death, my lady. They have no plans to let him see trial."

Surah let out a slow breath. "How did you come by this knowledge?"

"In the way that I come by all knowledge, my lady. I am a Watcher, as you well know. I believe it is the real reason your father has kept me around for so long. I see most all that goes on within the castle and city." He gave her a knowing smile, and Surah looked away.

Bassil's deep voice was just a whisper now. "You know I speak truth, princess."

"Who is behind it, Bassil? Who has given the word?"

"There are several, and I bet you could guess most of them, but that's not really what's important right now." The Warlock reached into his cloak and removed his sundial. He flipped the face open, looked at it, and flipped it shut again.

His dark face was deadly serious when he looked back up at her. "How did your Charlie put it? Time is…of the essence."

Surah stood from the bed and paced over to the window, where Samson still sat, his head raised, ears perked. "Why do you call him 'my Charlie'?" she asked. "That man is not mine."

Bassil's head tilted, and his white teeth flashed in a smile. "No?"

Surah threw her hands up, all the frustration and anxiety that had been building up the past two days snatching away her composure.

"Enough of this, Bassil. If you've got something to say, speak plainly. I am not in the mood for games. What is it you think, that I'm in love with the man?"

"I never said that, princess."

Surah placed a gloved hand on her hip, trying to keep the pink out of her cheeks. "Then what are you saying?"

Bassil sighed and stood. He went over to Surah and placed his large hands on her shoulders. "What I am saying, princess, is just what I said. I make no suggestions or accusations. What you do with the information is your decision. Forgive me, but I thought it would be of your interest. I may be wrong, but the point is, Charlie Redmine will not live to see the sunrise on this day if he remains where he is."

Surah looked over at Samson, and she knew the tiger could see plainly the horror in her lovely violet eyes. He had been mostly silent over the past couple days, as if brooding over something he hadn't bothered to tell her, and of course, he was. But he would always be there when she needed him. He was her North Star.

What he said was: *Like the moon loves the night and the sun loves the day.*

Surah did not know what to say to this, so she said nothing.

* * *

THAT EVENING, she found herself in the dungeons, standing outside Charlie Redmine's cell, having made up a lie to the Hunters standing guard about why she needed to see the prisoner.

When he looked up and saw her, his voice came out in a deep whisper. "Surah."

She came forward and gripped the bars of his cell . "Charlie," she breathed, releasing a long breath. She hadn't realized that she'd been worried she'd be too late until just this moment.

Charlie gave her a half smile, dimple appearing in his cheek. "You okay?" he asked.

She gave a quiet laugh, but it was ringed with anxiety. Her high cheekbones were flushed, and her heart was hammering in her chest. "You're asking me if *I'm* okay?" she said.

Charlie just looked at her, his shoulders relaxed, face calm. "What's going on?"

Surah spoke lowly and quickly, deciding to get on with it before she lost her nerve and changed her mind.

"That song you sang to break the spell, to free me," she said. "What was the name of it?"

Charlie's mouth tightened, and for a second she thought he was not going to answer. Then he looked down at his hands and spoke in a whisper, with more hesitancy in his voice than she had ever heard from him before, as if it pained him to say it.

"*Surah's Song*," he said. "It's called *Surah's Song*."

What he did next took her by utter surprise. His strong arms encircled her waist through the bars, sliding under her cloak and pulling her to him, pressing their bodies close together despite the metal separating them. His hand came up and lifted her chin, forcing her to look up into his green eyes.

Surah's mind raged at her to pull away, but her body leaned into him, her own hands coming up and lacing around his neck. His arms tightened around her waist, and she was glad for this because her knees were feeling less than sturdy. Her heart was thumping in her chest, her blood racing and rushing through her veins, and no matter how much she told herself she should stop this, she was powerless to do so. She didn't want to pull away. She didn't want the moment to end. She didn't want to let Charlie Redmine go. Not ever.

And it would have gone on longer. It would have lasted a lifetime, and in a way, she supposed it would. But, then, a voice spoke from the shadows outside the cell, and the moment was broken like shattered glass. She could almost hear the cracking.

The voice said only one word, but the cold, hard way it was spoken was enough for both Charlie and Surah to know the speaker instantly, and they looked over to see the gray eyes of the Head Hunter staring at them from the shadows beyond the cell.

Theodine Gray said, "Traitor."

Murderous anger laced his tone.

Surah did not allow herself time to think. She took Charlie Redmine's hand and wrapped her other around her sister's Stone that hung around her neck, a temporary replacement for the one she planned to get back from Charlie's brother.

Because she was sure she would be seeing Black Heart again. It was not over between them. No, she had a feeling it had only just begun.

She took a single deep breath and teleported Charlie out of there, the imprint of Theo's angry gray eyes stuck behind her lids like a flash of light.

Surah wondered what the hell she was doing as she held his hand tightly and they flew over space and time.

But once again, rather than flying, it felt more like falling.

She could only hope Charlie Redmine was also falling alongside her.

ABOUT THE AUTHOR

H. D. Gordon is the author of several fantasy series with strong female leads. She is the mother of two amazing daughters, and a lover of nature.

She believes our actions have ripple effects, and in the interconnectedness of all things.

H. D. spends her time with family, eating desserts, and taking strolls through the forests of New Jersey.

For more information visit:
www.hdgordonbooks.com

Moon of Shadows

Moon of Curses

<u>Academy of Witchcraft</u>

The Awakening

The Summoning